Escape from Sjór Borg

by Michael Eidam

Illustrated by Naoko Whitecavage

PUBLISHED BY

For Taylor Ann, Cade, Garrett, Raegan, and Ryan.

Chapter 1: Iceland

This isn't anything like the baseball fields back home, Ryan thought. It wasn't even *really* a baseball field. It was just a field with a small backstop and grass as far as the eye could see. No snack bar! Which meant no nachos. *Oh man, I want nachos!* he thought. He was lost in thoughts about melted cheese and tortilla chips when he heard his brother yell at him.

"Ryan, pay attention," Garrett said. He punched his baseball glove and turned toward home plate.

"Throw it as hard as you can," their cousin Cade told his father. Next year, Cade would be eligible to play in the majors with the older kids. They threw much harder and he wanted to be ready.

His father flashed a mischievous smile. "Okay, Cade, you asked for it." His dad didn't have much of an arm, but he could still throw faster than the average sixth grader. The next pitch whizzed by Cade before he even thought to swing. It smacked against the backstop and rolled halfway back to the pitcher's mound. "Strike one," his father said, flashing another smile.

Cade would not have admitted it (especially not to Taylor Ann) but the speed scared him a little. But only for a second. He refused to be afraid.

His father dug into the pitcher's mound with his foot. "It's the bottom of the ninth," he said. "Two outs. A man on third. A base hit wins the game."

Cade stepped back up to the plate and tapped it with his bat. *Eyes on the ball. No fear.*

***

Raegan heard a *doink* and looked up in time to see the baseball flying into the outfield and her cousin Cade running to first base. Her little brother Ryan was chasing down the ball. When he caught up to it, he tried to pick it up with his mitt.

"Ryan, use your hand," their older brother, Garrett, shouted. But Ryan ignored him and continued trying to pick it up with his glove. "Hurry!" Garrett yelled as he watched Cade round second base.

It took Ryan three tries before he was able to pick up the ball with his mitt. It looked like a scoop of ice cream on top of a cone. He grabbed the ball and threw it to Garrett. Well, not *to* Garrett. More like in Garrett's general direction. By the time Garrett got the ball, Cade had already crossed home plate and was jumping up and down triumphantly shouting, "Home run! Home run!"

Raegan was always being dragged to Garrett's baseball games, to his football games, to his basketball games. Now here she was halfway across the world in Iceland, and she was *still* being dragged to watch him and their cousin Cade play sports. In a couple of years, she would be going to Ryan's games, too. She didn't mind, though. She usually brought a blanket and a book to read. Her mother would tell her to stop reading and play with the other kids. Meanwhile, she was always telling Garrett to play less and read *more*. Parents. They never know what they want.

Ryan bounced over and tossed his baseball glove onto Raegan's blanket and copped a squat next to her. "What are you reading?" he asked. She normally read what she called chapter books but this one looked different. It had pictures. Ryan liked books with pictures.

"Stories about the Vikings," she said. "They used to live here." Raegan showed Ryan one of the pictures. It was a drawing of a wolf.

"Who's that?"

She had trouble pronouncing the name. "Fenrir. He's a giant wolf."

"Cool!"

Raegan turned the page and Ryan leaned over to get a better look at the next picture. He practically knocked her over.

"Ryan," she complained. "Give me space."

"Who's that?" he asked, pointing to the book.

She read the name. "Surt. He's a giant."

"Wow! Cool." Ryan looked at the picture of a giant holding a flaming sword, but then he grew bored. He noticed Cade and Garrett had begun tossing a football. "I get to rush the quarterback!" he shouted as he bounced up and ran to join them.

Raegan returned to her book. A few seconds later, her Uncle James sat down next to her. *He probably thinks I'm lonely,* she thought. But she didn't mind being alone. She never felt lonely when she was reading.

The next page was about dwarves, and the picture was a lot different than what she had seen in movies. According to the book, dwarves were black, so black you couldn't see them in the dark. They lived underground and if sunlight ever hit them, they would turn to stone.

"Uncle James?" she asked in her soft voice. "Do you think there are still dwarves living underground?

"I doubt it," he said.

"But how would anyone know if you can't see them?"

He nodded. "That's a good point." He looked at the drawing of two dwarves in her book. "Of course, if nobody can see them, then how do they know *that* is what they look like?"

Raegan looked at the drawing some more. "That's a good point," she said. Without looking at him she added, "You should put a jacket on, Uncle James. You're going to catch a cold." She turned the page and began reading about a giant sea serpent named Jormungand. He looked like a huge, wingless dragon!

Chapter 2: Sea City

A fire warmed the small cabin, and the light of its flames danced on the walls. There was so much equipment in the cabin, there was barely any room to walk around. Ryan picked up a scuba mask off the floor and put it on. It was way too big for him and just slid down his face and off his chin.

"Hand that to me please, sweetie?" his Auntie Jenn said.

Ryan took it off and handed it to her, and she packed it neatly in the case. Ryan was sad to see her packing because it meant Uncle James would leave for his adventure soon and the rest of them would have to go back home. He liked being in the cabin. Back home, everyone would be on their various devices playing video games or watching videos. But in the cabin, they had been playing board games and telling stories.

Ryan liked stories, especially the kind where everyone took turns telling a part of the story.

"What's that?" Ryan asked as his cousin, Taylor Ann, handed something to her mother. She was helping to sort and pack the gear.

"The regulator," she explained. "It's what enables you to breath underwater when you're scuba diving."

Her mother was about to pack it away when she paused, gave it a better look and grimaced. "Nice try," she said handing it back to Taylor Ann.

"I don't understand why I can't go with them. Dad's let me go before."

"That was in the Caribbean. This is the arctic rim. It'll be too dangerous."

"I'm not a kid anymore. I've been diving for over four years now. I can handle it."

"I've been diving for over twenty," her father said from the kitchen table, "and I'm not so sure *I* can handle it."

"That's comforting," Jenn said sarcastically.

"I'm not afraid," Taylor Ann said.

Her father stopped what he was doing for a moment. "It's okay to be afraid. It means you understand the risks. The trick is to not let the fear conquer you."

Ryan walked over to the kitchen table to see what his Uncle James was doing. He climbed up and stood on a chair to get a better look. There was a large map spread out on the table. It had lines drawn all over it and lots of writing, too.

Ryan watched Raegan on the chair next to him, copying the map in her journal. When she wasn't reading, Raegan was writing or drawing. He leaned over her to get a better look at the map.

"Ryan! Stop breathing on me," Raegan said. "Your breath stinks."

That made Ryan laugh. "I ate jerky!" he said and then he breathed in Raegan's face.

"Ew!" But rather than get upset, Raegan started laughing.

"Alright, you guys," their mother said as she made a plate of nachos in the kitchen. "What are we doing here, are we eating or are we looking at maps?"

"We're looking at maps!" Ryan said. He turned his attention back to the map. "What's that?" he asked pointing to what looked like a giant island.

"Iceland," his Uncle James answered.

"That's where we are!" Ryan pointed to another place on the map. "What's that?"

"Greenland."

Ryan pointed again. "What's that?"

"The Faroe Islands."

Ryan looked over the map. "Where are you going?"

"That's what I'm trying to figure out."

Ryan laughed. "If you don't know where you're going, how will you get there?"

"That's a good question, Ryan."

Ryan nodded. Sometimes adults didn't make any sense.

"If you don't know where you're going, then how can you know it's too dangerous for me?" Taylor Ann asked.

"It's the not knowing that makes it dangerous," her father answered.

"What are you looking for?" Garrett asked as he and Cade joined the others at the table. They all gathered around like it was story time.

"Sjór Borg," James said.

"She-yor borg?" Ryan said, trying to repeat the name. "That sounds weird."

"What does it mean?" Garrett asked.

"Sea City. According to the legend, the Vikings built a fortified city on an island in the Norwegian Sea. It was one of their most important trading posts until an earthquake caused the ground to fall out from underneath it and the city sank into the sea."

"Like Atlantis?" Taylor Ann asked.

"Except that Atlantis is fiction. Sjór Borg is supposed to be real. Some people believe the reason the Vikings were such great explorers is because they were searching for Sjór Borg. I plan to do what they never could. I plan to find it . . . *and* the treasure buried with it."

"What treasure?!" Ryan shouted excitedly.

"The Vikings were great warriors and plunderers. It's said they had a giant treasure room beneath the great hall in Sjór Borg. And when the city sank into the sea, the treasure was lost with it."

"I want to go with you!"

"Me, too!"

James knew better than to argue with them. Sure, they had been diving for years, but they had no idea what it would be like in *these* waters. "I'll tell you what: you can come with us on our way out to load the boat tomorrow, and when we're done, we'll do a test dive in the bay. If you can handle that, we'll take you with us."

"James!" Jenn shouted.

"Hey, they say they can handle arctic waters. Let's find out." He threw her a wink to let her know it would all work out.

"Can I go, too?" Ryan asked, turning to his mother.

"Maybe when you're older," she answered.

"Ugh. I'm *never* going to be older."

"We're just trying to keep you kids safe," his Auntie Jenn added, as much to Taylor Ann as to Ryan. "One day, you'll be old enough to understand that."

Chapter 3: The Beach

Taylor Ann stood on the beach, watching the waves crash against the rocks that dotted the shoreline. The sea was stormier than she expected. The wind blew the cold spray from the crashing waves into her face. It was much colder than she expected, too. She wasn't sure if she had ever felt water so cold that hadn't already been turned into ice. She was starting to get nervous. Maybe she *wasn't* ready.

She turned away and started back toward the sand dunes that rimmed the beach. Unlike the beaches back in Florida, this one was more muddy marsh than sand. She spotted Cade coming over the dune. He had the bag with his scuba gear slung over one shoulder, and his baseball bat resting on the other.

"Why did you bring your bat?" she asked.

"I don't know," Cade shrugged. "I always bring my bat." He dropped his bag next to hers at the bottom of the dunes. There was a dense fog in the air that hid anything more than ten feet away. They heard the others approaching before they could see them.

"Ryan, Mom said you can't come with us," Raegan scolded. "You're not old enough."

"When I was older I went scuba diving here all the time," he replied.

Taylor Ann and Cade watched as Ryan bounced over the sand dune dragging a fishnet bag with his snorkeling gear behind him. Unlike the others, Ryan was too young to scuba dive, so he didn't have his own air tank and regulator.

Raegan trailed after him. She had a backpack slung over her shoulders and was carrying another bag with her scuba equipment. She placed her scuba bag with the others.

"Why did we have to wake up so early?" Ryan whined as he plopped his fishnet bag on top of his sister's gear. Ryan hated waking up in the morning, and he hated waking up *early* in the morning even more.

"I didn't want to take a chance on them going without us," Taylor Ann explained.

One time, her father had promised to take her with him only to be gone when she woke up the next morning. "You promised I could go with you!" she had complained upon his return.

"You were asleep," he had replied.

"Why didn't you wake me up?"

"Why didn't you wake yourself up?"

She didn't have an answer for that. Her father was always teaching her to be self-reliant. Lesson learned.

Just then Garrett emerged into view carrying two bags. One had his scuba gear in it. The other belonged to Uncle James. He laid the two bags next to the others.

"What did you bring?" Cade asked.

Garrett unzipped the bag to show him: "Flashlights, glow sticks, canisters of Spare Air, rope, flares . . ."

"Nice!" Cade shouted. He dropped his bat and pulled out a speargun.

"Garrett," Raegan said disapprovingly. "That's Uncle James's bag."

"He's coming with us, Raegan. It's okay." Garrett never understood why Raegan was always trying to boss him around. She was his *younger* sister. But he knew better than to tell her not to be bossy. That only made her bossier.

Cade headed toward the water to see how cold it was when the ground rumbled. "What was that?" he asked, turning back to the others.

Ryan felt his stomach. "I think it was my tummy. I skipped breakfast."

"That wasn't your tummy," Garrett said. "That was the ground."

"The ground is hungry?"

The ground shook again, this time much more violently. "It's an earthquake," Cade said.

"Quick, duck and cover!" Raegan shouted, reflexively looking for a place to find cover.

"We're okay," Taylor Ann said. She was holding out her arms to help keep her balance. "The single biggest danger in an earthquake is being struck by flying debris," she said.

"What's debris?"

"It's a fancy word for stuff," Garrett explained.

Ryan pointed to their gear. "Isn't *that* stuff?"

No one answered him, but they all watched their gear. The ground was shaking so furiously their bags were actually moving. And then, as quickly as it had begun, it stopped.

"See?" Taylor Ann said. "I told you it would be okay."

Raegan blew a huge sigh of relief until she heard:

"Uh, guys, I think I'm sinking." They all looked over and noticed Cade had sunk up to his knees in the muddy sand.

"Stop screwing around, Cade," Taylor Ann said.

"I'm not screwing around. I'm sinking."

"Then stop sinking."

"How am I supposed to do that? I'm not trying to sink. It's just happening." He had sunk up to his thighs.

"It's quicksand!" Garrett said.

Chapter 4: The Quicksand

Garrett rushed to his Uncle James's bag and pulled out the rope. He tossed one end to Cade. "Here. Tie this around your waist."

"He's not going to sink," Taylor Ann said. "That's a bunch of Hollywood nonsense. Most quicksand is only a few feet deep." Taylor Ann took a step to help him and instantly sunk to her knees.

"You say that, and yet I'm still sinking," Cade replied. He managed to get the rope tied around his waist before sinking to his stomach. "Pull me out," he shouted to Garrett.

Garrett started pulling only to realize he had begun sinking, too. "I can't," he said. "I'm just pulling myself in."

Raegan rushed to Cade's bag and pulled out his mask and a canister of Spare Air. "Cade, catch!" she shouted. First, she tossed him the mask, then the Spare Air. By the time he got the mask on, he had sunk to his chest. "Taylor Ann!" Raegan said as she tossed Taylor Ann's mask and a canister of Spare Air to her.

"We're not going to sink," Taylor Ann said. "We'll touch solid ground any moment." But by this time, she had sunk to her stomach and was sounding a lot less confident than before. Then she sank some more. She quickly put on her mask and held the canister of air to her mouth.

"Raegan, grab mine," Garrett said. He had sunk to his knees. Raegan tossed him his mask and a canister of air.

"Here, Ryan," she shouted, tossing a canister of air to her youngest brother. Then she grabbed one for herself and pulled her mask out of her bag. Ryan nodded, and pulled his mask out of his mesh bag and put it on.

"Taylor Ann," Garrett said after putting on his mask. "Wrap the rope around you and then toss it back to me." He threw her his end of the rope. She wrapped it around her waist, then tossed it back. Garrett wrapped it around himself and then tossed it to Raegan. "Raegan," go up onto that hill." She grabbed the rope, but when she took a step towards the hill, her foot sank into the quicksand.

"Ryan," she shouted. "Take this rope up to that hill!"

Raegan wrapped the rope around her waist and then tried to throw the end to Ryan, but it fell short.

Ryan moved to get it, but Garrett shouted, "No! Don't come any closer!" Garrett took a moment to think things through. "Ryan, I want you to take off your jacket."

"He can't take off his jacket," Raegan said. "He'll catch a cold."

"Raegan!" Garrett said with growing frustration. "Let me handle this." He turned back to Ryan. "We need you to mark the spot where we sank so you can find it again. Okay? I want you to take off your jacket and leave it on the ground by your feet. Then I want you to—"

"Guys!" Cade shouted. He had sunk up to his neck. He put the canister of air to his mouth just before sinking completely out of view.

"Cade!" Taylor Ann screamed just before she sank, too.

"Ryan," Garrett said. "Leave your jacket on the ground and run and get—" Garrett felt the sand shift beneath him. "Go get—" He put the canister of air to his mouth just as the ground fell out from underneath him and he disappeared into the quicksand.

"Get *what*?!" Ryan yelled as he watched the sand close in over Garrett's head.

"Get Uncle James!" Raegan shouted a split second before the quicksand pulled her under, too, along with all of their scuba gear.

Ryan scowled at the area where the others had vanished. "Aw!" he complained. "But I want to go with you!" It wasn't fair. They were always leaving him behind.

The ground shook again, more violently than before, and Ryan fell on his bum. The muddy sand around him began pouring down into a huge hole like water down a drain. It swept Ryan up in its current. *I guess the ground* was *hungry*, he thought as the stream of muddy sand carried him toward what looked like a giant mouth. He put the canister of air to his lips right before the ground swallowed him whole. All the nearby quicksand rushed in after him and filled the hole completely.

Several moments passed, and all that could be heard was the sound of waves crashing against the rocks. A seagull let out a cry that filled the morning air. It landed on the beach where, just moments before, five kids had stood with their scuba equipment, waiting to go diving. Only now there was no sign they were ever there.

Chapter 5: The Mudslide

Ryan could feel himself sliding and gliding down. It reminded him of the water slide park at home, only instead of sliding on top of water, he was sliding inside a bunch of mud. Mud was all around him. He could feel the mud flowing over his legs, his chest, his cheeks and ears. It was moving so fast, it was pulling off his mask. He buried his chin into his chest like he did at the water park to keep the water from going up his nose. He held the canister of air tight to his mouth with both hands to make sure the mud didn't get in. He didn't want to breath mud. That would be gross.

This wasn't like the slides Ryan liked at the water park. He liked the ones that whipped him left and right around sharp turns. This was like the giant slide that went straight down, really, really fast. He wasn't allowed to go on that one. They told him he was too short. He told them he could do it, but they wouldn't listen. Adults never listened. They were always telling him he wasn't old enough or big enough to do things. They would have told him he wasn't big enough to go sliding down a mud tunnel, too, but here he was, sliding down and down and down.

And down. Ryan was starting to worry. It seemed to go on forever. How far down could he go? How would he ever get back up again? But then he noticed he wasn't going down anymore; he was going forward. Instead of being inside the mud, he could feel himself floating on top of it, like it was a river.

And then he stopped entirely. "Is it over?" he asked.

"Ryan, is that you?! Where are you?"

It was his sister, Raegan. Ryan looked around, but he couldn't see anything. "In the dark," he answered.

"That's not very helpful," Raegan said.

Ryan heard a pop, and then a soft green light emerged. Garrett had found the bag with the glow sticks. He handed one to Raegan. "Come over here, Ryan."

"That was fun!" Ryan shouted as he stood up. "Can we do it again?!" He tried to rush over to them, but his feet got stuck in the mud and he tripped and fell on his face. He lifted his head with a mouth full of mud. *Gross*. It took him several tries to spit out all the mud, and then he was over it. He stood up again and waded toward the group. "Raegan did you see how fast I was going?"

"It was completely dark, Ryan. How could I see you?"

"I was going a hundred miles an hour!"

"You weren't going *that* fast."

"How do you know? You couldn't see me."

"Here you go, Ryan," Garrett said. He had tied a loop of string to one of the glow sticks and draped it around Ryan's neck. The stick hung glowing at his chest.

"I'm like Iron Man!"

"Just keep it on so we can see you, okay, bud."

"Okay."

Raegan took off her backpack and held the glow stick to it like a lantern. The backpack was all gross and muddy. But it was waterproof, so she knew the things inside it would be okay. She originally wanted to bring her Hello Kitty backpack. That was her favorite. But since they were going on a boat, she brought her waterproof backpack. It wasn't as cute as her Hello Kitty backpack—it was blue-green like the ocean, not pink—but it was more practical.

She unzipped the small section of the backpack and pulled out a packet of wipes. She wiped the mud off her fingers, and then unzipped the larger section to make sure all her things were okay. She had brought her journal, some snacks, sandwiches, and juice packs, and the book about Norse mythology in case she got bored and wanted to read. They were all okay. She sighed in relief. She was proud of herself for preparing so well. The others never prepare for anything, but she came prepared.

Cade and Taylor Ann joined the group, and Garrett handed them each a glow stick. Cade was winding the rope back up. He handed it to Garrett who put it back in the bag with the other gear.

"Now what do we do?" Cade asked.

Taylor Ann held her glow stick up to get a better look at their surroundings. They were trapped in an underground cave. "Find a way out," she said.

Chapter 6: The Cave

Garrett pulled a flashlight out of the gear bag and handed it to Taylor Ann. He took another one for himself, and they started painting the cave walls with light.

"I found a tunnel!" Garrett shouted, rushing toward its entrance. It wasn't very high or wide. It looked like it had been built for kids instead of adults. He aimed his flashlight down the tunnel, but it didn't reveal much; the darkness inside was so thick it easily beat back the light.

"What's that?" Ryan asked. He pointed to a symbol carved into the stone next to the tunnel's entrance.

"It looks like a dragon breathing fire," Raegan said. She pulled out her journal and, by the light of her glow stick, began drawing a picture of the dragon.

"There's another tunnel over here," Taylor Ann said. She shined her light on the symbol next to the tunnel's opening. "What do you think it is?" she asked.

"It looks like a rock with something in the middle of it," Cade said. "A diamond maybe?"

Taylor Ann took several steps down the tunnel before stopping. "This tunnel goes down," she called over her shoulder. "If we're going to get out of here, we need to go up." She reemerged from the tunnel and continued searching the cave.

Raegan, with her journal still in hand, crossed over to the second tunnel to draw a picture of the diamond-rock symbol. Ryan watched the glow sticks and flashlights bounce around the otherwise dark cave.

"Hey, my bat!" Cade exclaimed.

Taylor Ann pointed her flashlight in time to see Cade pull his bat out of a huge pile of sandy mud. "This must be where we came in," she said as she lit the edges around the mud pile. "It's a third tunnel."

"Or *was*," Cade said, shaking the mud off his bat.

"Does it have a symbol?" Garrett called out from the other side of the cave.

Taylor Ann searched the edges of the tunnel with her flashlight until she found what looked like an O carved in the stone.

"What do you think it means?" Raegan asked as she approached and began drawing the stone O.

Taylor Ann examined the symbol more closely. It was just a circle. *What could that mean?* she wondered. She would have assumed it was an O if the other symbols were letters, but they were pictures. So this must be a picture of something, too. But what? And then it came to her. "I bet it means exit," she said. She turned and gave Cade a worried look: *The exit is blocked!*

"Did you find any more tunnels?" Cade asked as Garrett joined them.

Garrett shook his head. "We have two options," he said, shining his light on each option as he spoke. "The diamond tunnel . . . and the dragon tunnel."

"Well, we don't want to go down," Cade said. "So I guess we should take that one." He pointed to the symbol of the fire-breathing dragon.

"The dragon tunnel?!" Raegan said. Although she didn't use the actual words, her tone said, *That is crazy talk!*

"Maybe we should stay here," Taylor Ann suggested. "Dad will come looking for us." She was still pointing her light at the tunnel where they came in.

"Yeah, but how will he find us?" Cade said. "The tunnel is completely blocked."

"The radio!" Garrett said. He searched through his Uncle James's bag and pulled out a small communication device that attaches to a scuba mask. He put it back and continued searching until he found a hand-held radio. He turned it on and pressed the talk button. "Hello, can anyone hear me?!"

"Let me try," Taylor Ann said. She took the radio and changed the channel. "Channel sixteen is for emergencies," she explained. "Mayday! Mayday! Can anyone read me?"

The radio hissed and crackled.

She pressed the talk button again. "Mayday! Mayday! Is anyone hearing this?!" Again, there was no response. She tried another channel. "Mayday! Mayday!" She waited a moment, then looked at the others and shook her head. "We must be too far underground."

"We're on our own," Cade said.

Garrett took the radio from Taylor Ann and put it back in the bag. "You *are* always saying you want to be an explorer," he said. "Well, here's your chance."

Taylor Ann felt a tingle of nerves. Exploring always sounded exciting and fun, but if they couldn't find a way out, they might *die* down here. There was nothing fun about that. What if they get lost in the tunnels? What if her father does come but they're no longer here?

The ground started to rumble again, softly at first. Ryan grabbed his stomach. "Oh, man. I am *so* hungry."

"That was the ground, Ryan."

"It's going to eat us *again*?!"

"It's an aftershock," Taylor Ann said with alarm.

The rumbling grew, and more sandy mud began flowing into the cave. It came slowly at first, but then rushed in faster and faster. If they waited much longer, it would fill the entire cave and bury them alive! They didn't have a choice.

"Come on!" Garrett yelled. "Grab your gear and let's get out of here."

The mud was starting to gather deep around their feet, rising almost to their knees. It was making it harder to walk. They grabbed their bags and headed for the dragon tunnel. The ground rumbled again, more violently this time, and they heard what sounded like an explosion of mud bursting into the cave.

"Run!" Raegan shouted.

They ran as fast as they could down the dragon tunnel with the thunderous roar of gushing mud bearing down on them. They didn't dare look back.

Chapter 7: The Dragon Tunnel

Deep inside the tunnel, the sound of rushing mud faded and they felt safe enough to stop running. Which was a good thing, Ryan thought, because he was starting to feel winded.

They walked quietly for several moments before Raegan broke the silence. "This is crazy!" she said. "Who goes *toward* a dragon?"

"Knights would go searching for dragons all the time," Garrett said. "You of all people should know that. *You're* the one reading all the time."

"Yeah, but they were *knights*. They had swords and shields. We're just kids. What do *we* do if a dragon comes?" She stopped walking as if to say she wouldn't go any further until someone answered her question. The others stopped with her.

CHAPTER 7: THE DRAGON TUNNEL

"I'll fight it," Cade said finally. He held his bat like a sword.

"Me too," Ryan said, jumping into a karate stance. He was pretty sure dragons didn't know karate, and he knew a little, so he would have an advantage.

"You're going to fight the dragon with karate?" Garrett asked with a chuckle.

"Yup. I'm going to kick him in the weenuts."

"You're not supposed to kick people in their privates, Ryan," Raegan said.

"It's okay if they're a stranger." Ryan looked down the dark tunnel. "And I don't know this dragon."

"Come on," Taylor Ann said. "There is not going to be a dragon."

They resumed walking before Garrett said, "Right. And we're not going to sink in quicksand."

"What does that have to do with it?" Taylor Ann turned and flashed her light accusingly in Garrett's face.

"I'm just saying you were wrong about the quicksand. Maybe you're wrong about this, too."

"*I* wasn't wrong about the quicksand. The *TV show* I saw about quicksand was wrong. Besides, quicksand is a real thing. There's no such thing as dragons."

"If there's no such thing as dragons, then what are we talking about?"

"What?"

"Are we talking about nothing? Or are we talking about dragons?"

"We're talking about dragons," Ryan said with a wrinkled brow. He didn't understand how Garrett forget so easily.

"I rest my case."

"Okay, fine. There is such a thing as dragons. But they're not real."

"So you were wrong. Again."

"I wasn't *wrong*."

"You said there was no such thing as dragons. Now you admit there is. So you were wrong."

"You know what I meant."

"Stop!" Cade shouted. At first, they thought he wanted them to stop arguing, but as Taylor Ann turned to face forward, she noticed her flashlight was no longer shining off the tunnel walls. Instead, its light disappeared into darkness. She shined the light down at her feet and realized she was standing on the edge of a cliff. One more step and she would have fallen into nothingness.

Chapter 8: The Dragon Pit

It took Taylor Ann a moment to catch her breath. She slowly stepped back from the edge, still shaking.

"Are you okay?" Garrett asked, putting his arm around her shoulder. She nodded. "That was close," he added as he looked toward the edge.

"Now what do we do?" Cade asked, shining his light into the darkness.

"We can't go back," Garrett said. "The cave is going to be completely filled with mud."

"Well, we can't go forward, either."

"Why would the tunnel just end at a cliff?" Taylor Ann said after she had conquered her fear. "That doesn't make any sense." She crept to the edge and peered into the abyss for a long moment. "Wait a minute," she said, finally. "Cade, turn off your flashlight." She turned off her light and Cade did the same.

The others joined her, but Garrett forced Raegan and Ryan back. "Stay away from the edge, okay, you guys."

"Put your glow sticks away, too," Taylor Ann suggested. She took the glow stick off from around her neck and put it in her pocket. Garrett and Cade did the same. "Do you see that?" she asked.

"See what? What are you guys looking at?" Ryan whined, unable to see past them.

"Something is glowing down there."

"What do you think it is?" Cade asked.

Taylor Ann turned on her flashlight and aimed it towards the glow, but the beam wasn't strong enough to reach it.

"I know," Garrett said. He went back to their gear. After searching through one of the bags for several seconds, he returned holding a flare gun. "Look out," he said, and the others gave him room at the edge.

Garrett fired the flare out into the darkness, and a moment later it erupted in a flash of red light. They saw what looked like an enormous cave. The flickering light from the flare made it look like the cave walls were burning. "What *is* this place?" Garrett said.

"A dragon pit," Cade suggested.

"Dragon pit?!" Raegan yelled.

"It's not a dragon pit," Taylor Ann said. "It's a volcano. That's lava. See it? That's what was glowing."

"Oh, great," Garrett said dryly. "So we're trapped in a volcano with burning lava. I'm not sure that's better."

"Look!" Cade said, pointing across the volcano. "There's another tunnel over there."

"Where?"

"All the way across on the other side. Do you see it?"

"A lot of good it does us all the way over there." Garrett said.

"I could jump over there," Ryan suggested. He had joined them at the edge without them noticing.

"It's too far to jump, Ryan."

"I could make it."

"No, you wouldn't. You'd fall down into the volcano."

"I won't fall. I'll make it. When I was older, I made that jump all the time."

Ryan walked away, and the others figured he had given up on the idea of jumping—except for Raegan. She kept her eyes on him as he sifted through their gear. "What are you doing, Ryan?"

He was tying the rope around his waist. "I'm going to get us out of here," he growled with determination.

"Ryan, you can't—" But before she could finish, he was past her, running as fast as he could. "Ryan, no!"

The others turned to look, but before they realized what he was doing, before they even *thought* to grab him, he had reached the edge, and just as the light of the flare died out, he jumped out into the darkness and disappeared.

"Ryan!"

Chapter 9: The Roar

Their screams echoed with growing softness off the volcano walls. *"Ryan . . . Ryan . . . Ryan."*

Raegan could feel tears rushing to her eyes. "Ryan!" she shouted again.

"What?" he answered as if he was annoyed with her nagging him.

Upon hearing his voice, Cade got down on his stomach and crawled to the very edge. "I can see his glow stick," he said. He inched further out, and Garrett held down his legs just to be safe. Cade aimed his flashlight straight down over the edge.

There, on a ledge below, Ryan stood looking up at him and smiling. "I told you I could make it," he said.

Taylor Ann was so relieved, she didn't bother correcting him.

"And, see?" Ryan continued, pointing down toward his feet. "I found a path. But you guys should take the ladder because I skinned my knee when I jumped and it *stings*."

"What ladder?" Cade asked. He felt along the edge until his hand closed on a metal bar. "There's a ladder!"

They gathered their equipment and climbed over the edge and down the ladder. They found Ryan sitting against the wall that ran along the path. "Did you guys feel another earthquake?" he asked.

"No."

"Then my tummy is definitely grumbling. I'm *so* hungry!"

"I told you not to skip breakfast," Raegan said as she took off her backpack.

"I wasn't going to wake up even *earlier*."

"Here," Raegan said. She pulled a snack pack out of her bag and handed it to him.

"Thank you, Raegan."

Raegan smiled. If it wasn't for her, they'd probably all *starve*. The others sat down around her, and Raegan handed them each a snack pack and juice box. There were two extras, one each for Uncle James and Auntie Jenn. That made her sad. They were all supposed to go scuba diving, but instead they were stuck inside a *volcano* of all places.

When they were all done eating, Raegan collected their trash in a plastic bag she had brought for just that purpose. *Even if this is a volcano, we shouldn't litter*, she thought as she tied up the bag and put it in her backpack.

Cade was the first to stand. "We should keep going," he said as he grabbed his bag and slung it over his shoulder. The others grabbed their things, too, and they all started down the path.

They had been walking for several minutes before Garrett said, "Do you guys notice something?"

"What?"

"We're going *down*."

"I thought we wanted to go up," Ryan said.

"We do."

"It's not like we have any choice," Taylor Ann said.

"If we go back, we'll be going up," Ryan said, just trying to help.

"Yeah, but if we go back, we'll be going backwards," Cade explained. "And we need to go forward."

Ryan cocked his head and furrowed his brow. He wasn't sure if that made sense.

"It's hot in here," Garrett said.

"Well, it *is* a volcano," Taylor Ann said.

Garrett just rolled his eyes. He loved his cousin, but he didn't love it when she acted like a know-it-all. *You can't sink in quicksand. Dragons don't exist. It* is *a volcano*, he was thinking when a vicious roar shot out from the darkness.

"What was that?" Raegan asked.

Cade put down his bag and gripped his bat with both hands. "It sounded like . . . a *dragon*."

Upon hearing the word 'dragon,' Ryan jumped into his karate stance, and his eyes darted wildly to and fro, on the look-out for winged monsters.

"It can't be a *dragon*," Garrett said in a mocking tone. "*Dragons* don't exist."

"That's a relief," Raegan said.

"I was being sarcastic, Raegan." Garrett turned to Taylor Ann and gave her a knowing look.

"What?" Taylor Ann protested. "You don't *know* it's a dragon."

"Maybe not," Cade interrupted. "But I know I don't like the sound of it. Come on. Let's get a move on." He grabbed his bag and rushed down the path, and the others rushed after him.

You're not going to eat me, Dragon, Ryan thought as his legs carried him as fast as they could.

Another screeching roar filled the sky. It was even louder than the first one, and it echoed throughout the volcano. When the echo finally died down, they heard the sound of flapping wings above them.

"He's coming!" Raegan yelled.

"There's a tunnel up ahead," Cade shouted. "Come on!"

Chapter 10: The Farting Tunnel

Cade reached the tunnel and threw his bag inside. He stayed out front, guarding the entrance with his flashlight in one hand and his bat in the other, on the look-out for winged enemies. "Hurry!" he shouted as he waved the others inside.

Cade waited for them to pass by, and then he backed his way toward the entrance, his eyes still searching the sky above him. As he turned to enter the tunnel, his flashlight caught a symbol carved into the wall.

"Did you guys see the symbol?" he asked as he grabbed his bag and joined the others. "It was the same one from the cave. A rock with a diamond in the middle."

"Great," Garrett said. "We went into a volcano for nothing."

"It's okay, Garrett," Ryan said. "I had fun."

"Fun?!" Raegan exclaimed. "We were just chased by a dragon!"

"I'm sure it wasn't a dragon," Taylor Ann said.

"Whatever it is, next time I'm going to kick him in the weenuts," Ryan added.

"Wait a minute," Cade said. "If that *was* a dragon, then that means there might really be diamonds up ahead!"

Diamonds! they all thought. Their eyes widened with excitement and their steps quickened and they hurried to find what awaited them at the end of the tunnel.

Raegan noticed Ryan was limping a little. "Is your knee okay?" she asked.

He looked down and checked his scrape. There was a small trickle of blood running down his leg. "I'll live," he said, mimicking what his mother probably would have told him.

"Here. Let me clean it," Raegan said. Ryan stopped, and Raegan took off her backpack and knelt down.

The others waited as she took out an antiseptic wipe and a band-aid.

"You brought a first aid kit?" Cade asked.

"Of course."

Ryan watched as she pressed the two sticky ends of the Spider-Man band-aid to his knee. He nodded in approval. "Thank you, Raegan."

She kissed it the way their mother would have done, then she packed up her kit, threw her backpack on, and they all continued on their way.

The further they walked into the tunnel, the more they noticed a noxious smell. It was so putrid, they couldn't help but cough. Garrett pulled out the front of his shirt and buried his nose in it. "Ryan, did you fart?" he asked.

"I don't think so."

"It's gas," Taylor Ann said, covering her nose with her blouse. "It's coming from the tunnel."

Ryan started to laugh. "The ground ate us and we gave it gas," he said. Then he grew angry. "Serves it right," he growled.

The air started to grow colder and eventually the light from their flashlights stopped bouncing off the walls, and they realized they had entered a large opening.

"Ugh," Raegan complained. "It smells even worse in here."

"This must be the tunnel's butt," Ryan said. Then he laughed at his explanation before thinking about it some more. "Ew, gross. We're in its *butt*?!"

"Tunnels don't have butts," Raegan said.

"Then how is it farting so much?" he argued.

"There are gases trapped in the rock," Taylor Ann explained. "When you dig tunnels like this it can release the gases into the air."

Cade aimed his flashlight at the ceiling where it set off hundreds of sparkling little lights. "Can those be stars?" he wondered.

"I don't think so," Taylor Ann answered. "The smell is too strong for us to have made it outside."

Garrett set down his bags and pulled out the flare gun.

"Not here," Taylor Ann cautioned. "The gas might be flammable." She searched their surroundings with her flashlight until she caught sight of what looked like a cart. "I know what this is. It's a mine."

"A diamond mine!" Cade said, still looking up at the 'stars.' "Those are diamonds up there."

"They might as well be stars," Garrett said. "There's no way for us to get up there."

"There's a tunnel," Taylor Ann said as she followed her flashlight's beam over to the mine's wall. She scanned the wall with her flashlight. "And another one. And *another* one. They're all over the place."

"So which one do we take?"

Her flashlight danced from one tunnel to another before she turned to Cade and Garrett with a worried look. She didn't know; there were too many.

Chapter 11: The Diamond Mine

"I don't think these tunnels lead anywhere," Taylor Ann said. They don't have symbols. The other tunnels had symbols to mark where they led. Like street signs."

"They have symbols," Raegan said. She was in the middle of drawing a picture. "See?" She pointed to a line and two dots carved in the rock next to the tunnel.

"What do you think it means?" Cade asked.

Taylor Ann moved to the next tunnel. It had a line with three dots. The next one had a line with four dots, and the one after that had two lines. "They're numbers," she said.

"These must be mine shafts, and this is how they numbered them. A dot means one. A line means five. This is number ten."

Taylor Ann stopped outside one of the mine shafts. "Okay, this is mine shaft one." She called out the numbers as she continued along the circular wall of the mine. "And this is two . . . three . . . four . . . five—that's where we came in . . . six . . . seven . . . eight . . . nine . . . ten . . . zero . . ." She slowed down as she realized she had come full circle. "And back to one." She stopped and returned to the last shaft. "Why would they number one of them zero?" She wondered.

"That's not a zero," Cade said, approaching. "That's the same symbol as before. This is the exit!"

"Not anymore," Garrett said. "The exit caved in, remember? This will just take us back to where we started." There was a moment of silence before Garrett added what they were all thinking. "I think we're trapped in here."

"We can't stay here much longer," Taylor Ann said with a cough. "There's too much gas. It will make us sick."

Ryan watched as they frantically searched the mine shafts again to make sure they didn't miss a way out. They were starting to look worried, Ryan noticed. "Why don't we just take the stairs?" he said, trying to help.

"What stairs?"

"These stairs." Ryan was sitting on the second step of a stone staircase. He pointed down to the first step. "There's a symbol."

Cade flashed his light on the bottom step to reveal a hammer symbol carved into the stone. Garrett and Raegan joined him, and Raegan began drawing a picture of the hammer in her journal. Ryan looked over to where Taylor Ann still stood in the middle of the mine. She looked sad.

"I went all the way around," she said. "How did I walk *right by* a giant staircase?"

"Probably because you were looking for tunnels and not stairs," Ryan answered. "But I wasn't looking for any more tunnels. I am *sick and tired* of tunnels."

Up until that moment, Taylor Ann was starting to feel more confident about their ability to find a way out. But now she was starting to doubt herself again. Ryan was right. She was only seeing what she wanted to see, and not seeing what was really there. *Some explorer.* She needed to do better. She needed to keep both her eyes and her mind open. She joined the other kids at the bottom of the staircase.

Cade aimed his flashlight up the stairs, but he was unable to see the top. "Where do you think they go?" he asked.

"They go up," Ryan explained.

Chapter 12: The Forge

Ryan bounced to his feet and began the climb, but after several steps, he started to slow and eventually the others passed him. "How much longer," he complained? "My legs are *killing* me!"

"We're almost there," Cade answered.

The stairs went up in a circle, rounding the mine twice before they reached an open archway at the top. The same hammer symbol from the first step was carved into the stone next to the archway. The kids entered.

***

The hammer room was much smaller than the mine. In the middle was a large anvil with a fat-headed hammer and tongs resting top of it. Next to the anvil was a large iron pot. "It's a forge," Taylor Ann said as she inspected the hammer and tongs.

"What's a forge?" Ryan asked.

"It's where you make things. Like pick axes and shovels. This must be where the miners made all of their tools."

"And swords," Cade added. He was standing by a table with a sword suspended at each end by two U-shaped clamps.

"I want a sword!" Ryan yelled as he rushed over.

"It doesn't have a handle," Garrett noticed. "They must have never finished it."

"Aw, man!" Ryan threw his arms into the air as if it was the end of the world.

"They were letting it cool," Cade said as he inspected the blade. "It's not polished, either."

"Why would miners make swords?" Taylor Ann asked, more to herself than to the others.

"To fight the dragons that don't exist," Garrett answered in a half-mocking tone.

Taylor Ann just rolled her eyes and began scanning the walls with her flashlight. Garrett grabbed the other flashlight from where Cade placed it on the table and began searching the other end of the forge.

Ryan became bored with the unfinished sword. He looked around and noticed his sister was sitting on the floor with her journal. "What are you drawing?" he asked as he sat down next to her.

"A map. See?" She pointed out the various places as she spoke. "This is where we came in. And this is the tunnel we took to the volcano. This is the volcano," she explained, tracing a large circle with her finger. "And this is the path we followed to the tunnel that led to the mine."

"Is that where I jumped?" he asked, pointing to where the tunnel met the path.

"Yeah, but you shouldn't have done that," she said, still looking at the map. "This is the tunnel to the mine, and this is the mine, and these are the stairs we took up to where we are now."

Cade finished inspecting the sword and walked over to where Taylor Ann's flashlight had stopped before another tunnel. The same symbol they saw outside the dragon tunnel was carved into the wall.

"I bet it leads to that tunnel we saw on the other side of the dragon pit," Cade said.

"It wasn't a *dragon pit*. It was a *volcano*."

"Whatever," Garrett said as he passed by. "Cade is probably right, which means it's a dead end." He continued searching.

"There could be another path below it," Taylor Ann continued, "like the one before. Or it could intersect with another tunnel."

"Maybe," Garrett said as he scanned the walls with his flashlight.

Taylor Ann took a few steps down the dragon tunnel, then looked back to Cade who stayed waiting for her. Her eyes seemed to ask him to side with her and try the dragon tunnel.

But before he could say anything, Garrett shouted, "I found another tunnel." His flashlight was shining on the tunnel's symbol.

"It looks like a triple-layered cake," Cade said.

"I think someone's hungry," Taylor Ann said.

"*I* am," Ryan said.

"You're always hungry, Ryan," Raegan said as she began to draw a picture of the symbol in her journal.

"I know," Ryan said with full seriousness as if it was a heavy burden he carried.

Taylor Ann flashed her light into the tunnel. It led up a steep, narrow staircase. Cade, holding his bat, was the first one up the steps.

***

"Where are we?" Taylor Ann asked as they climbed out of the narrow staircase and into the dark. The beams from their flashlights shined on nothing but darkness. Either they were outside, or inside something very, very big.

In answer to her question, Garrett shot a flare into the air. It burst into a flash of red light that colored their entire surroundings.

Cade's mouth almost dropped to the ground. "It's a stadium," he said as he gazed up at a row of seats that lined a high wall. "Like where gladiators would fight."

"Whoa!" Ryan said. He took off running as if he were in a one-man chariot race.

"Ryan, be careful," Raegan shouted after him.

"When I was older, I fought in this stadium all the time," he shouted back. He jumped into his karate stance and started punching and kicking the air.

Rather than chase after him, Raegan sat cross-legged on the ground and began drawing a picture of the stadium in her journal.

"This isn't just a stadium," Taylor Ann said. "Look." She pointed toward the far end where they could barely make out a giant stone wall. As she approached, more came into view: towers, battlements, and an iron gate. "That wasn't a picture of a *cake*," she said. "It was a castle."

Chapter 13: The Secret City

As Taylor Ann continued to take in their surroundings, she realized the stadium served a defensive purpose as well. Its walls extended from the castle and continued all the way back to where the entrance to the mine had been dug into the rock mountain. So if an enemy came this way, they would be trapped within the two walls. However, there were also several rows of seats along the walls, so people could sit and watch whatever was happening on the ground. *These people were more than just miners,* she thought as the light from the flare died away and returned everything to darkness.

She followed Garrett's flashlight to where Garrett and Cade stood outside the castle's main gate. They could enter its archway about three feet before the iron gate blocked their path. Cade grabbed its bottom rung like it was a barbell and tried to lift it, but the gate was too heavy.

"Dead end," Garrett told Taylor Ann. "Did you see any other way out?"

She shook her head. "How high do you think that wall is?" They walked out of the archway and looked up at the wall that towered above their heads.

"Too high," Cade said.

Garrett examined the openings in the wall's battlements, also called embrasures. "I got an idea," he said. He rushed back to their gear and returned carrying the rope. "Cade, let me see your bat." Cade handed it over and Garrett tied the rope in a knot around the center of the bat. Then he took a couple of steps back and tossed his flashlight to Cade. "Shine a light on that opening up there." Cade aimed the flashlight, and Garrett grabbed the bat like it was a javelin and tossed it into the opening.

The loud crack of aluminum hitting stone echoed loudly throughout the stadium. Garrett pulled on the rope, and because he had tied it to the bat's center, the bat came back lengthwise and stopped against the sides of the opening; it was too long to fit through it. He pulled on the rope a couple more times to make sure it would hold. "We'll climb up," he said.

Garrett planted his feet against the wall and, using the rope to pull himself up, began 'walking' up the wall. When he reached the top, he crawled through the opening. "Bring over the gear first, and then, Cade, you come up next," he called down.

Cade and Taylor Ann brought all their bags to the foot of the wall. Cade climbed up next. Then Taylor Ann tied the rope around one of their bags and Garrett pulled it up. He and Cade took turns hauling up their bags, one by one.

"Okay, Ryan, your turn," Taylor Ann said. She tied the rope around his waist. "Just in case," she explained.

Ryan clapped his hands together. "Let's do this!" he said. He grabbed the rope with determination and powered his way up the wall with a grunt. It was a good thing Taylor Ann had tied the rope around him, because half way up his foot slipped and he slammed face-first into the wall. Without the rope, he would have fallen.

Cade and Garrett pulled him the rest of the way up, and when he finally got to the top, they noticed his lip was bruised and bleeding. "You okay?" Cade asked.

"What a *day* I'm having."

Cade chuckled and rubbed his head, and then all three of them helped pull Raegan up even though she insisted she could climb up herself. Taylor Ann was the last one up. Cade untied the rope from the bat and handed it to Garrett, who slipped the rope back into the bag. Cade rested his bat on his shoulders, grabbed his gear and headed toward the tower at the far corner. The others grabbed their things and followed him.

When they got there, Garrett shined his light through a tower window, but it found nothing but darkness. He shot another flare into the sky and it revealed the inside of a huge cave, almost as if they were inside a hollow mountain. The castle sat atop a cliff that was *at least* hundreds of feet high. They couldn't tell for sure because it simply disappeared into darkness. The cliff seemed to be floating in the middle of a dark, silent sea.

"How far down do you think it goes?" Taylor Ann asked.

Garrett grabbed a glow stick from the gear bag and tossed it over the side. It never hit bottom, but just disappeared beneath the sea of darkness.

"Let's check the other side," Taylor Ann suggested. They grabbed their things and hurried along the wall to the tower at the opposite end. Garrett shot another flare into the sky only to reveal more of the same. The castle rested on a giant cliff with a sea of darkness below it, and a hollow mountain above.

"Guys, look," Raegan said. They turned and, for the first time, looked the other way—toward the inside of the walls. Down below, basking in the red light of the flare, was an entire city.

"Whoa!" Ryan said.

The main street led to a great hall that dominated the city. Several other structures surrounded it, including one that towered into the air with a tall, sloping roof. It looked like the building was wearing four pointy hats, one on top of the other. But as much as they intended to survey the whole city, their eyes kept returning to the great hall; it had a majestic quality that demanded their attention. A moment passed with no one uttering a word, until:

"Do you guys hear something?" Garrett asked. "It sounds like . . . wind."

"That's me breathing," Ryan said. "I'm so *tired*." There was a moment of silence, and then they heard a screaming roar. "Okay, *that* wasn't me," Ryan said.

"The dragon," Raegan said, and Ryan instinctively went into his karate stance.

"Maybe we should keep moving," Taylor Ann said. When the others looked at her in surprise, she added, "Not because I think it's really a *dragon*. Because they don't exist."

As if the dragon wanted to argue the point, it roared again from out of the darkness. This roar was louder. Closer. The silence that followed was filled with the sound of flapping wings.

"How do we get down?"

"This way." Cade led them along the battlements toward another tower halfway down the length of the wall. Inside was a staircase leading down to the ground floor. As they descended the stairs, they heard flapping wings circling above them.

"Wait," Garrett said. They all huddled together under the archway at the bottom of the stairs. "It's right above us."

"It's not a dra—"

But before Taylor Ann could finish the sentence, they heard a whoosh and a stream of fire lit the sky. And on the ground in front of them, just for a split second, they saw the enormous shadow of a winged creature. The shadow's mouth opened, revealing dagger-like teeth, and another screeching roar thundered from above.

Chapter 14: The Armory

"There's a door to the right," Cade said, peeking around the corner of the archway. "When I say go, run for it as fast as you can."

"I am *sick and tired* of running," Ryan said. "I thought we were going to *fight* the dragon."

"Ryan," Garrett said with little patience. "Don't argue."

Raegan wasn't taking any chances. She grabbed her little brother's hand to make sure he wouldn't be left behind.

Cade peeked out from under the tunnel and flashed his light into the sky. He could hear the wings, but they sounded further away, yet coming closer as if the dragon was circling back toward them. This was their chance. "Go!" he yelled.

They all ran as fast as they could into the doorway. Once inside, they breathed a sigh of relief. "Let's stay in here for a little while," Taylor Ann said. "Wait for that thing—whatever it is—to leave."

"Guys, check it out," Garrett said. The beam of his flashlight revealed a row of stalls, like the kind you find in a locker room. Only, instead of baseball or football gear, these stalls were filled with armor, spears, swords, and shields.

"Cool!" Ryan exclaimed.

"This looks like a Viking helmet," Cade said as he took a helmet from one of the stalls.

Raegan sat down and began drawing pictures of all the weapons. She had seen most of them in her book on Norse mythology, but that was a book. This was real life!

"Huh?" Taylor Ann said as she inspected a suit of armor. "Shouldn't this all be rusted or corroded in some way? It almost looks . . ."

"New," Garrett said.

"But how is that possible? Unless . . ."

"The Vikings are still down here. Making weapons."

"Small Vikings," Cade said. He had taken down a breastplate and was holding it to his chest. "Look, it almost fits."

"With big heads," Ryan added. He had tried on a helmet and it was covering his entire head. It made his voice sound distant and metallic.

Cade returned the breastplate and grabbed a sword. It wasn't very big, almost like it was made for a kid his size.

"I want a sword," Ryan said as he took off the helmet.

"No, Ryan. They're too dangerous and you're too small," Raegan said without looking up from her drawing.

"They're *kid*-sized," he argued.

"They're still too sharp," Garrett said. "Sorry, buddy."

"Tell you what," Cade said as he sheathed his sword, and wrapped the belt around his waist. "You can take my bat." He grabbed his bat from where it rested in the stall and handed it to Ryan.

"Cool!" Ryan grabbed the bat and then growled and swung it as hard as he could at one of the breastplates hanging in a stall. He hit the breastplate with such force, the bat bounced right back and hit him smack between the eyes. He wobbled and fell on his bum.

Garrett and Cade just laughed, but Raegan rushed to his side. "Ryan, are you okay?"

It took a moment for the shock to wear off. He rubbed his forehead and sucked in a breath between closed teeth. "What a *day* I'm having," he said.

"I told you, you're too little," Raegan said.

"I am *not* too little!"

Garrett knelt down in front of him. "You need to control your anger, Ryan." He shined the light on Ryan's forehead. "How many fingers am I holding up?" he asked.

"I don't know, it's dark in here."

Garrett aimed the flashlight at his own hand.

"One," Ryan answered.

"You'll have a bump, but you'll be okay."

Ryan got back on his feet and picked up the bat. He looked at the breastplate and his anger started to rise. He growled, reared the bat and was about to strike again when Garrett caught the bat. "Let's just call it a tie, okay, buddy?"

Ryan huffed and puffed, but eventually he nodded.

"There's another exit over here," Taylor Ann called from the other end of the room.

Cade grabbed the shield from the same stall where he got his sword, and then grabbed the spear. Garrett grabbed the sword, shield, and spear from the stall next to him, and they exited slowly, their flashlights searching the sky, their ears listening for the sound of flapping wings.

Once the others had left, Ryan turned back to the enemy breastplate and growled. He swung his bat in a downward motion and it banged against the breastplate with a loud metallic clang. The breastplate fell from its hook and landed on the floor by his feet with a pained clink. "Serves you right," he said, pointing the bat at his fallen enemy. Then he followed the others out with the bat slung over his shoulder thinking, *You're next, Dragon.*

***

Stone booths lined each side of the main street leading into the heart of the city. "I bet these were stores," Taylor Ann suggested as she peeked over a front counter. "This must have been their marketplace."

Where the booths ended, the street opened into a large courtyard in front of the great hall. To each side, slightly behind the hall, were two other structures.

"That one is probably the keep where they lived," Taylor Ann explained as she lit the building with her flashlight. "And that one looks like a temple," she added as she shined her light on the building with the tall sloping roof.

Without saying it, though, they all seemed to know they were going into the great hall. The three older kids climbed the stairs leading to its front door, while Raegan sat down on the bottom step and began drawing a picture of the great hall. Ryan sat down next to her.

"Why are you drawing everything?" he asked.

"I don't know," she said. Raegan wanted to be an explorer someday, too, but she knew it was about more than just adventure. You needed to study maps, chart a course, and take good notes. What was the point of exploring if you didn't remember anything? You needed to take good notes so you could share your discoveries with others.

Ryan looked up toward the great hall. The others were at the top of the stairs trying to get the door open. Cade was pulling on it as hard as he could, but it wasn't opening. Ryan turned back to watch his sister draw some more. She was really good. When she drew something, it looked like the thing she was drawing. Whenever he drew something it didn't look anything like anything. That's why he didn't draw very often.

"I'm hungry," he said.

"You're always hungry."

"I *know*."

Raegan could hear Cade and Garrett grunting, followed by the groaning of wood and the squeaking of hinges. The door was opening. She knew she didn't have much time left, so she hurried to finish her drawing. *There's never enough time,* she thought.

Then she heard Taylor Ann scream.

Chapter 15: The Dwarves

Raegan stuffed her journal into her backpack, and she and Ryan rushed up the steps. Taylor Ann was trying to catch her breath, but she was also chuckling. Raegan looked past her to see a stone statue standing in the middle of the doorway. It had an angry-looking snarl on its face, like it was yelling at them, and it held its hand out as if telling them to stop.

"Are you okay?" Raegan asked.

"It just startled me," Taylor Ann said. "What an odd place to put a statue," she added. "In the middle of the front door?"

"He looks like he's telling people to keep out," Cade said.

"He reminds me of you, Raegan," Garrett added with a teasing smile. "Bossy."

That made Raegan scowl.

"It's a weird statue, too," Taylor Ann said. "Look, the statue itself is made of stone, but the clothes are . . ." she felt the fabric ". . . real. And just like the armor, they look new."

"His pose is weird, too," Cade added. "Almost like he was frozen in mid-action."

"Oh, no!" Raegan exclaimed. She pulled out her book on Norse mythology, flipped to the page on dwarves, and handed it to Taylor Ann. "Dwarves lived underground because if they got caught in sunlight, they would turn to stone," Raegan explained. "What if this is not a statue? What if it's a *real* dwarf who was turned to stone?"

"Those are just stories, Raegan. Myths," Taylor Ann said as she handed the book back to her.

"Besides, there's no sunlight down here," Garrett added.

"Not now," Raegan said. "But there could have been a long time ago."

"We *are* inside a volcano," Cade added. "Who knows, the mountain could have blown its top before caving back in on itself, letting sunlight in just long enough to freeze him."

They all looked at the statue for a long moment, and then Garrett turned to Taylor Ann and said, "I guess this is where you tell us there is no such thing as dwarves." Taylor Ann just rolled her eyes and continued into the hall.

Raegan and Ryan continued to examine the statue, and Raegan drew a portrait as she studied it. He was only a little taller than their brother Garrett, but taller than she thought a dwarf was supposed to be. He looked young for a dwarf, too. His shoulders and arms were big like a football player, and he wore thick gloves over large hands. His beard covered the lower half of his face, so only the skin around his nose and eyes was showing. The stone was dark. She wasn't sure what kind of rock it was, but it was nothing like the marble statues in Greece and Rome which were always white. His clothes were black, too. It was difficult to see exactly what he was wearing in the dark.

"I don't think you look like him," Ryan said. "You don't even have a beard."

"Gee, thanks," Raegan said.

"There are more over here," Taylor Ann called out. At the far end of the hall, there was a large table with six dwarves sitting at it. They were all looking at the doorway, and one of them looked like he was shouting to the dwarf by the door.

"This one looks grumpy," Cade said.

"Grumpy dwarf. Why does that sound familiar?" Garrett asked.

"Snow White and the Seven Dwarves," Taylor Ann answered.

"Oh. Right."

"Wait. A. Minute!" Ryan said. He counted them aloud: "One, two, three, four, five, six . . ." then he pointed to the one at the door ". . . seven! There are seven dwarves."

An eerie feeling washed over Taylor Ann, but she shook it off. "I'm sure that's just a coincidence," she said.

"I guess," Ryan said. He considered the scene some more, and the sight of a dinner table made his stomach grumble. "I'm hungry," he whined.

"Me, too," Cade said.

"I'm thirsty," Garrett added.

They all looked expectantly at Raegan. She plopped her bag down on the table and sat in the only open chair. She unzipped her backpack and pulled out seven sandwiches, two snack packs, and nine juice boxes. "This is all I have left," she said.

"What would we do without you, Raegan?" Cade said.

"Starve."

"Well, then it's a good thing you're here," he said with a pat on the back. He grabbed a sandwich and juice box before adding, "Thanks, Raegan."

The others all stopped by to grab a sandwich and a drink, each one thanking Raegan, and then they disappeared into the dark hall to explore.

Raegan put the extra food away and then opened her journal. She drew portraits of the dwarves sitting at the table as she ate. She started with the one who looked like he was shouting. He looked like the oldest and Raegan guessed he was probably the leader. "I'm sorry the sun turned you into stone," she said as she drew his portrait. Raegan lost herself in her drawing, so much so that she had drawn three of the dwarves before she realized something was different. They were looking at her!

She could have sworn they were all looking at the door before. *Weren't they?* But now they were definitely looking at her. *You're imagining things,* she told herself. After drawing the last dwarf, she updated her map, lost in her own world until she heard:

"Let me in!" It was Ryan's voice coming from the side of the great hall. She quickly packed up her things and rushed toward him.

When she arrived, the others were there too. Ryan was standing in front of a stone statue that was blocking a narrow doorway. "You better let me in, Dwarf!" he yelled.

The statue looked very familiar. Raegan pulled out her journal and compared this dwarf to her drawing of the one blocking the front door. "He looks just like the other dwarf," she said, but no one answered her.

Ryan banged his bat on the ground twice before shouting, "If you don't move, I'll *make* you move."

"Ryan, don't hit the statue," Raegan said. "It could be a frozen dwarf."

"I don't care. He's being mean."

"He's not being mean. He's being statuesque," Garrett said with a chuckle.

"Fine. I'll move him." Ryan dropped his bat and went to pick up the statue.

"Ryan, you can't lift that," Taylor Ann said. "It's solid stone. It probably weighs—" But before Taylor Ann could finish, Ryan picked up the statue like it was nothing more than a large stuffed animal and moved it out of the way. Taylor Ann gasped in astonishment. She turned to Garrett. "How did he do that? It doesn't make any sense."

"Does any of this make sense?" Garrett said before following his little brother through the narrow doorway.

Taylor Ann turned to Raegan. "That statue should weigh hundreds of pounds."

"*If* it's a statue," Raegan answered. "Maybe frozen dwarves weigh a lot less than stone." She trailed after her brothers.

"It's not a frozen dwarf," Taylor Ann mumbled. She turned to Cade for support. "Right?"

But Cade's mind was elsewhere. "Look," he said, shining his light on the symbol next to the doorway. It looked like a treasure chest in the center of a maze. He smiled and rushed after the others.

Chapter 16: The Treasure Room

After only ten steps, Ryan stopped at an intersection. "It's a maze," Cade explained as he caught up to them.

"So which way?" Garrett asked. "Left, right, or straight?"

"Let's go right."

They started to walk off, but Raegan called out, "Wait." She took a piece of chalk out of her backpack and drew an arrow on the floor pointing in the direction they were going.

"Good thinking, Raegan," Garrett said.

Raegan smiled. She got the idea from a book she read. It was a good thing she brought her chalk with her. She almost didn't bring it. *Why would I need chalk on a boat?* she thought. But then she thought, *Why not bring it just in case?* So she did.

At the next intersection they took a left turn. Then another left. Then a right. At every turn, Raegan drew an arrow on the floor to mark the way they went, but this wasn't like any maze she had read about in books. It didn't just go left, right, or straight. It went up and down too. They took several turns before they saw one of her arrows drawn on the floor and knew they had double-backed. Raegan drew an X over the original arrow, then drew another arrow leading in the opposite direction, and the group headed that way. They did this several times for what felt like an hour. After dozens of turns—both wrong turns and rights turns—they found themselves at the top of a narrow staircase with nowhere else to go but down.

They descended the stairs, and at the bottom found themselves in a room about the size of a basketball court. Piled high in the middle of the room was a mountain of treasure: gold coins, silver coins, diamonds and jewels of all colors—blue, green, red, and white—piled as high as their flashlights could shine.

"Whoa!" Ryan said.

"How do we get it out of here?" Cade asked as he watched Ryan grab two handfuls of jewels and dump them into the pockets of his cargo shorts.

"Maybe we should go back for our gear bags," Taylor Ann said.

Garrett pulled a sack of gold from the treasure mountain. "We can use these sacks," he said. He dumped some of the gold out and began gathering diamonds, rubies, sapphires, pearls, and other jewels to put in the sack.

Cade grabbed a sack, and as he began filling it with treasure, he wondered if he would have enough to buy a pro baseball team. He would buy the Angels, and then his dad wouldn't need to go all over the world exploring. They could manage the team together and go to every game together!

After Garrett finished filling his first sack, he unzipped Raegan's backpack, stuffed the sack inside, and went to fill another one.

"You guys," Raegan said. "We shouldn't take this. It's not ours."

"This is how exploring works," Cade said. "We found this treasure and now we get to keep it."

"It would be different if people still lived here," Taylor Ann added as she filled her own treasure sack.

"What about the dwarves?"

"You mean the *statues* of dwarves? Raegan, if not for us, this treasure—this whole city—would stay lost down here forever."

Raegan looked down like she was still not convinced. She didn't offer any more argument, but she decided *she* wouldn't take anything. Instead, she sat down on the ground and drew a picture of the mountain of treasure.

When the others had gathered as much loot as they could carry, they left the treasure room and, using Raegan's arrows on the ground as a guide, made their way out of the maze and back into the hall. They were so excited, none of them noticed that the dwarf by the door was no longer there.

The kids all dumped their treasure sacks onto the large table and began taking inventory of all their gold and jewels. They were at it for several minutes before Raegan realized something was different. Except for the treasure, the table was empty. The stone dwarves were gone.

"Uh, guys . . ." she said ". . . where did all the statues go?" The others were too excited counting their riches to hear her. "Hey!" Raegan shouted. "Where are all the dwarves?!"

Ryan was the first one to look up, scan the table, and realize she was right. "They're gone!" he said.

Chapter 17: Trapped!

The others came out of their treasure-crazy trance. "Someone else must be in here," Cade said. He backed away from the table and pulled his sword out of its sheath. Garrett did the same. They searched the hall with their flashlights. Raegan watched the beams sweep across the great hall looking for clues. Then, the lights stopped by the front door.

"Over here," Garrett called. The others joined Garrett and Cade at the front. There, the same dwarf who told them not to enter, who guarded the entrance to the treasure room, that same dwarf was now blocking their way out. He held his right hand out with an open palm facing up, and with his left hand he pointed to the far corner of the hall.

"He's pointing that way," Cade said. "Come on." Cade held his drawn sword in front of him and swept the area with his flashlight as he made his way to the far end of the hall.

The other kids followed, but Raegan stayed and looked at the dwarf some more. *Why is his hand out?* she wondered. *It's like he wants something.*

"Get out of our way!" she heard Ryan yell from the far end of the hall. She went to see what was going on. Where the two walls should have met to form a corner, there was a narrow passageway between them instead. A dwarf was blocking the way and pointing in the other direction, back toward the first dwarf. "Move or I'll move you," Ryan threatened.

"He sounds like *you* talking to *him*," Cade whispered to Garrett. That made Garrett chuckle.

The stone statue didn't respond which just made Ryan angrier. He huffed, then growled, then went to pick the statue up.

"Wait!" Raegan shouted. "They want us to give them something first." She rushed back to the statue by the front door.

"Raegan, they're *statues*," Taylor Ann called after her. She looked to Cade and Garrett with an expression that said, *This is crazy.*

"Just go with it," Garrett said.

When Raegan arrived at the first dwarf, she knew she was right. His right palm was still out and his left hand was still pointing to the far corner, but his expression was totally different. He almost looked *pleased*, like he was *proud* of her.

"See?" she told the others once they arrived. "He has one hand out like he wants something, and with the other hand he's pointing the way. He wants to trade. If we give them what they want, they'll show us the way out!"

"So what do you think he wants?" Garrett asked.

Raegan studied the statue more closely. He appeared to be looking at something. She followed his line of vision to where it landed on Cade's treasure sack. "He wants his treasure back," she realized.

"He's not getting it back," Cade said, protecting his sack. "We found it. It's ours now."

"Do you want to get out of here or not?"

Garrett turned to Taylor Ann. "It's just a statue, right? So give him *your* treasure."

"We don't have time for this," she protested.

"Go on," Garrett continued. "If he's just a statue, your bag of treasure will stay right there in his stone hands." Then he added in a mocking tone, "Unless you think he's *real*."

Taylor Ann rolled her eyes and went to put her treasure sack on the dwarf's hand, but the bag was too big to fit, and it started falling off. So instead she hung the drawstring over his open hand. "There," she said. "Happy now?"

"Come on!" Raegan shouted as she ran to the second dwarf.

When they got there, the dwarf was standing off to the side with one hand pointing down the open passageway, and the other extended outward waiting for more treasure.

They all traded wide-eyed looks that seemed to say, *Spooky*.

"We should get our stuff," Cade said.

They all ran to their gear, except for Taylor Ann who ran to the front door. The statue she gave her treasure to was no longer there. "It's gone!" she shouted. She returned to the group in absolute shock. "He's . . . he's *gone*." But the smug look on Garrett's face helped her snap out of it. She grabbed her gear. "That still doesn't mean he's *real*. It could mean someone else is in here playing a trick on us."

Ryan looked all around to see if he could find someone watching them.

"Maybe," Garrett said. "Or maybe you were just wrong. *Again.*"

Ryan took Taylor Ann by the hand and started leading her toward the second dwarf. "It's okay to be wrong," he said. "What's important is that you learn from it."

Taylor Ann was pretty sure she had said that same exact thing to Ryan not too long ago. And now *he's* the one teaching *her? What the heck is going on here?!* she wondered. When they reached the second dwarf, without even being told, Ryan hung his bag of treasure on the dwarf's hand the same way Taylor Ann had done before, and the group made their way down the dark passageway.

The tunnel was so narrow they had to walk single file. Cade led the way with a shield and spear in hand. At his request, Taylor Ann aimed the flashlight over his shoulder lighting their way. Garrett guarded their rear with his sword at the ready. The tunnel sloped down, and they kept making left turns, going further and further down. The air was getting hotter and more stifling. They had been walking for almost twenty minutes before they arrived at a narrow staircase, even more narrow than the tunnel. It led straight down.

"Guys," Cade said, "what if they're not showing us the way out? What if this is a trap? What if they're just leading us down to their *dungeon* or something."

Several seconds of silence passed before Ryan answered him. "Then I'll kick them in the weenuts!"

"We've come this far," Taylor Ann said reassuringly.

Cade sighed and nodded. He turned sideways to fit inside the tight passageway, then slowly began down the stairs. Down and down they went, and the air became hotter and hotter.

Chapter 18: The Cliff

Finally, they emerged from the staircase onto a narrow ledge. A dwarf was there, blocking their way to the left and pointing to their right. Other than the ledge, the rock wall behind them, and the dwarf, there was nothing but darkness.

Garrett shot a flare into the air and everything came into view. The narrow ledge ran along the middle of a cliff. The cliff wall towered hundreds of feet above them and, on top of it, they could see the walls of the castle and one of its towers. Below them, the cliff disappeared into a sea of darkness. They looked to where the dwarf was pointing. Far off in the distance, at the end of the ledge, were two more dwarves. One of them was pointing out into the void. The light from the flare died away, and the dwarves disappeared back into the darkness.

"Oh, great," Garrett said. "They're telling us to jump off the cliff."

"Again?!" Ryan complained. "I already did that!"

Taylor Ann inched her way towards the other dwarves to investigate. She followed his finger with her flashlight. She didn't see it at first, but eventually her light found something that appeared to cross the void. "There's a bridge here," she said. The bridge had been painted black to make it invisible in the darkness.

The others joined her. "Where does it go?" Garrett asked.

Taylor Ann aimed her flashlight across the bridge, but the beam wasn't strong enough to reach the other end. They had no idea how long the bridge was, or where it went. "It's not like we have any other options," she said.

Garrett looked at the dwarf's open hand, then to Cade. But Cade had stepped away to inspect the bridge. Garrett sighed, took his treasure sack out of his gear bag and gave it to the dwarf. Then, they carefully began to make their way across the bridge.

Only Raegan noticed that the second dwarf was holding out a helmet like he wanted them to take it. She reached out slowly and put both hands on the helmet. She looked at the dwarf's face for any clue she was doing the right thing. She tugged on the helmet and it came away from his hands easily. Not knowing what else to do, she put it on, and followed the others.

The bridge was made of rope with wooden planks to walk across, like the bridges Raegan had seen in movies or read about in books. She had never seen one in real life before, though, and she had definitely never had to cross one before. She watched her feet carefully to make sure they found the wooden planks and didn't fall through the cracks, which wasn't easy because she was wearing a helmet that was way too big for her and made it difficult to see. Plus, the planks were painted black. So was the rope. She could barely see anything. She kept her hands on the two side ropes at all times to be safe. "Be careful, Ryan," she said instinctively.

She couldn't see her brother, but she could hear him huff in the darkness. "When I was older, I crossed this bridge all the time."

"Really?" Garrett asked. "Then where does it go?"

"To the other side," Ryan answered.

They had not walked much further before Cade heard the familiar sound of flapping wings. "Do you guys hear that?" he asked.

"Hear what?"

As if in answer to the question, a thunderous roar rained down on them. They all paused.

"The dragon," Cade said.

"That doesn't exist," Garrett added.

"You're not funny," Taylor Ann said.

In the darkness, they heard Ryan growl. "This dragon is becoming a real pest."

They heard another roar, only this time it wasn't coming from above. It was coming from right in front of them! Cade raised his shield and readied his spear.

Chapter 19: The Dragon

They felt something land on the bridge. Only, whatever it was, it didn't seem to be very heavy. "Taylor Ann, light," Cade said.

She flashed the light over his shoulder, but all it revealed was more empty bridge. Cade inched his way forward. There was another roar, and it echoed in the darkness. He was getting close. He steadied his nerves and continued going forward until finally, the flashlight's beam settled on the dragon. A real-life dragon! A very *small* dragon.

"It's the size of a puppy!" Cade said with a laugh.

"Well, look at that," Garrett said. "A dragon. I guess Taylor Ann was wrong again."

"That's not a dragon. It's too small."

"Two hours ago, you said there was no such thing as dragons. Now you're an expert on how big they are?"

The dragon roared again, and they could feel the force of it on their faces like a hot wind.

"How can such a *small* creature make such a *loud* noise?" Taylor Ann wondered.

"He reminds me of you, Ryan," Garrett said.

Ryan nodded, but then furrowed his brow. He wasn't sure if that was a compliment or not.

The dragon roared again. "Well, there he is, Ryan," Cade said. "Go kick him in the weenuts."

Ryan made his way to the front of the group, studied the dragon for a moment, and then hopped into his karate stance which made the whole bridge sway.

"Ryan, be careful!" Raegan shouted from the back.

"Get out of our way, Dragon," Ryan said, "or I will *kick* you in the *weenuts*." The dragon just growled, and Ryan growled right back at him. When the dragon didn't move, Ryan demonstrated a few of his karate chops before adding, "I'm warning you, Dragon! Are you going to get out of our way or not?"

The dragon cocked his head and wrinkled his brow like he was trying to make sense of Ryan's antics, and then he said something. At least Ryan thought he said something. But he had no idea *what* he said because he didn't recognize any of the words. He knew it wasn't a roar, and it definitely wasn't a growl. Now it was Ryan's turn to cock his head and furrow his brow. "I think he's talking to me," he said.

"He's not *talking*," Taylor Ann said. "He's just making noises with his mouth."

"Isn't that what talking is?"

Raegan, still wearing the helmet, made her way to the front and stood beside her little brother. "He wants us to pay the toll," she said.

"How do you know that?"

"Because he just said it."

"No he didn't. He said something like, 'Borga gald.' Whatever that means."

"Exactly," Raegan said. "Pay the toll."

The dragon snorted.

"What's the toll?" Raegan asked.

The dragon spoke again, and after he finished, Raegan nodded and unzipped her backpack.

"You understood him?" Cade asked.

"You couldn't?" She thought about it for a moment. "Maybe it's the helmet," she said. *"That's* why the dwarf wanted me to take it!"

"Ask him why he's so small," Garrett suggested. But the dragon answered him without waiting for Raegan to repeat the question.

"He says he's not small," Raegan said. "He's actually big for his age." She pulled a snack pack out of her bag, opened it, and placed it on the bridge before the dragon. The dragon devoured it like he hadn't eaten for centuries.

"He even eats like Ryan," Garrett said as he watched the dragon chomp on the food.

"Those snack packs are *good*," Ryan said in the dragon's defense.

When he finished, the dragon burped and a spurt of fire shot out of his mouth. Then he farted and another spurt of fire shot out of his bum.

"Definitely reminds me of Ryan," Garrett said.

Ryan knew *that* wasn't a compliment and it made him scowl.

The dragon said something else, then flew away, roaring into the dark. "He said we can pass," Raegan explained.

The kids crossed the remainder of the bridge to find two more dwarves waiting for them. One had both of his hands out like he wanted something placed in them. Raegan gave him the helmet. "Thank you," she said.

The other dwarf was holding out one hand and pointing with his other. Cade looked to Garrett, then to Taylor Ann. "We already gave them ours," she said.

"Fine." Cade pulled his treasure sack from his bag and gave it to the dwarf. *There goes my baseball team*, he thought.

Garrett looked to where the dwarf was pointing. "It looks like a forest," he said.

"A forest?" Taylor Ann wondered. "How can trees grow in here without water or sunlight?"

Chapter 20: The Petrified Forest

The trees were not like anything they had ever seen before. They looked more like scary stone statues of trees than actual trees. Taylor Ann ran her hand along one to feel its surface. "They're petrified," she explained.

"What does that mean?" Ryan asked.

"They've turned into stone."

"Like the dwarves," Raegan said.

"Are we going to turn into stone, too?!" Ryan asked.

"These trees have probably been here for hundreds if not thousands of years. We're not going to be here that long."

"I wouldn't be so sure of that?" Garrett said. "This forest seems to go on forever."

Raegan kept hearing noises like footsteps behind her. She slowed her pace, and then as quickly as she could, she turned around hoping to catch one of the dwarves following them. But all she saw were petrified trees. She continued walking, and again she heard footsteps. She jumped around to face the other way, but again there was nothing but trees behind her. She was about to turn back when she got a funny feeling. One tree looked like it was the same distance behind her as it was before she had taken her last several steps. *That tree should be further away,* she thought. She turned around and deliberately counted off five steps, and then spun around as quickly as she could. The tree was right in front of her. "Guys," Raegan said, "I think the trees are following us."

"That doesn't make any sense," Taylor Ann said.

"You're still trying to make sense of all this?" Garrett replied.

"Hold on," Raegan said. They all turned to watch as she pulled chalk out of her backpack and marked each nearby tree with a letter going all the way up to F. When they turned back around, they got the creepy sensation that the trees in front of them had somehow gotten closer while they were turned the other way. In fact, all the trees looked like they were closing in on them. There was only a narrow path to their right through which they could escape to a nearby clearing.

"Listen," Cade said. "When I say go, run as fast as you can to that clearing. Is everyone ready?" They all nodded. He took a deep breath. "Go!"

They ran as fast as they could into the clearing and then Cade yelled, "Stop! Everyone, form a circle, back to back." They did, all being sure to keep their eyes on the trees around them.

"Look!" Ryan shouted. He pointed to a tree at the edge of the clearing. On its stone trunk was the letter F written in Raegan's handwriting.

"They *are* following us," Raegan said.

"I think they're trying to trap us," Garrett said. He turned around and noticed the trees in front of them were closer than they were just seconds ago.

"I don't think they can move while we're looking at them," Cade said. "So stay in a circle, and everyone look at the trees in front of you so they can't close in on us."

"And what, just stand here staring at trees for the rest of our lives?" Taylor Ann said. "We need to keep moving."

"Yeah, but in which direction?" Garrett asked.

"Light a flare," Cade suggested.

Garrett started digging in his bag. "I only have two left," he said. "Maybe we should save them." When he looked up, he noticed the petrified trees had managed to sneak closer while he was looking in his bag.

"We need to see better to find the way out," Taylor Ann said.

And then, as if in answer to her call, they saw what looked like a shooting star coming towards them out of the darkness. As it got closer, they saw it wasn't a star at all, but a boar with golden fur that shone like the sun. The boar was running toward them—actually running on the air! It landed within the clearing, right in front of Ryan. It grunted, and Ryan grunted back. It grunted again, and Ryan replied with another grunt. It was like they were talking to each other.

"Well, Ryan, what's he saying?" Garrett asked.

"He wants us to follow him."

Taylor Ann was pretty sure Ryan didn't *really* just have a conversation with the boar, but she figured, at this point, following a glowing pig was as good a plan as any. "Alright, Boar," she said. "Show us the way." Garrett gave her a shocked look and she just shrugged. "When in Rome," she said. To their surprise, the boar grunted as if it understood and then took off running.

The kids ran after it, being sure to look behind them every so often to stop the trees from closing in on them. Eventually, the number of trees started to thin out and they came to a clearing next to a river. The boar ran out into the middle of the river, turned back toward them and snorted, then took off running down the river, actually running on the water! With his retreat, the boar took his golden fur and its light with him, returning the petrified forest to darkness.

"What do you think?" Taylor Ann asked. "Should we go after him?"

"He took off too fast for us to follow him," Garrett said. "Maybe we're supposed to cross here." He looked back and noticed the trees were still following them. "Raegan, Ryan, keep your eyes on those trees, and don't let them get any closer."

They nodded and turned to watch the trees. Ryan stared at them so angrily he looked like he was trying to shoot them with laser beams from his eyes.

Taylor Ann knew Garrett's comment made perfect sense under the circumstances; that's why it annoyed her so much. *Stone dwarves, puppy-sized dragons, moving petrified trees trying to trap us . . . what's next?!* she wondered.

"Maybe we should follow the river to its source?" Cade said. "It could be the way out?" He took a few steps upriver when they heard a loud snarl, then a great growl, and then an outrageous roar, followed by the sound of approaching thunder. The ground began to shake so violently that Ryan fell on his backside.

"It's another earthquake!" Garrett shouted.

But then the rumbling slowed as the sound approached closer. Boom. Boom. Boom. It was as if the ground itself was a drum being played by a giant drummer. Boom. Boom. Boom. Then it stopped.

Cade aimed his flashlight toward the sound. There, on the faint edges of the light, were two great columns made of fur, one on each side of the river. "What are those?" he wondered. He aimed the light downward to where the furry columns ended in giant paws with enormous claws. Then he aimed the flashlight up into the air where the beam barely revealed a gigantic snout. The snout was coming towards him. Cade took a step back, then another. "Keep the light on it," he said as he tossed the flashlight to Taylor Ann. He raised his shield and readied his spear, just as the full head of a gigantic wolf came into view.

Of course, Taylor Ann thought. *A giant wolf comes next.*

Chapter 21: The Giant Wolf

The wolf's mouth was wide open and its lips were pulled back in a snarl, revealing its monstrous fangs. The mouth was so large Cade could have walked right up the tongue and not even bumped his head on the top row of teeth. But the wolf couldn't close his jaws because a large sword was keeping them pried open. The wolf was drooling enormous amounts of saliva and the kids realized the river was made of his drool.

"His *mouth* is the river's source?!" Garrett said. "I'm pretty sure that's not the way out," he added sarcastically.

The wolf sniffed at Cade, and then howled with full fury. Cade hid behind his shield as the wolf sprayed him with an angry wind of spittle and bad breath. It was like being caught in a smelly hurricane.

Raegan thought her cousin was a goner until she realized the wolf couldn't come any closer. A leash so thin it looked like fishing line was holding it back. The wolf growled and scraped its claws against the ground as it tried with all its might to get closer to Cade, but he was out of reach.

When they realized Cade was safe, they all breathed a sigh of relief. "Maybe we should go *that* way," Cade said, pointing in the opposite direction.

"Good idea."

They walked down the river with the giant wolf growling and snarling behind them. Only Ryan looked back at him. *He didn't look so tough*, Ryan thought.

As he walked, Ryan was looking backward more than he was looking forward. He wanted to make sure the stone trees didn't sneak up on them. *I'm sick and tired of those trees*, he was thinking when he bumped into Raegan and realized the others had stopped. He turned around and saw all seven of the stone dwarves standing in front of them.

Two of the dwarves looked like they were holding up shields, only they had no shields. Two more looked like they were thrusting spears, but they held no spears. Another dwarf looked like it was about to draw his sword, but he had no sword.

What are they doing, Raegan wondered, and then she realized, "They want their weapons back."

"They can have their shield," Cade said as he laid it at a dwarf's foot. The wolf's slobber was still dripping off it.

Gross, Raegan thought.

Cade seemed less willing to give up his sword and spear, but after Garrett dropped his weapons, Cade dropped his, too.

The head dwarf was holding something that looked like a slab of engraved wood. Taylor Ann went to take it from him, but she couldn't get it out of his hands.

"Here, I'll do it," Cade said. He pulled on it with all his might, but it didn't budge. "Help me, Garrett." Even with the two of them pulling as hard as they could, they couldn't pry it out of the dwarf's hands.

"Maybe it's not for us," Garrett suggested.

"Or maybe he still wants something?" Taylor Ann said.

"Yeah, but what?" Cade asked.

"I'll do it," Ryan said as he pushed Cade and Garrett to the side and stepped between them. He pulled on the wooden slab with all his strength. He grunted loudly like he believed grunting would make him even stronger. However, his hands

gave way before the dwarf's and Ryan slipped and fell on his butt. He popped up and got in the dwarf's face. "Don't make me angry, Dwarf!" he warned. He tried again to wrest the wooden slab away, but no matter how hard he pulled or how much he grunted, it wouldn't budge.

As Raegan watched her brother struggle, she noticed the dwarf seemed to be looking at her. She waited for Ryan to tire himself out.

"It's impossible!" he groaned, tossing his arms into the air.

He stepped aside, and Raegan approached the dwarf. She looked into his eyes, and then gently reached for the wooden slab. She imagined the dwarf was smiling at her. Raegan pulled ever so slightly and the wooden slab came away easily.

"How did you do that!" Ryan shouted.

"He must have wanted *you* to have it," Garrett said.

"What is it?" Taylor Ann asked.

Raegan turned it over and on the other side was an elaborate map carved into the wood. It showed the mountain where the mine was, the city, the great hall, the petrified forest, the river, and several other areas they never saw. A path with arrows showed them the way out. "It's a map!" she said. She looked up into the stone dwarf's eyes. "Thank you."

Taylor Ann took the map and looked it over. "If I'm reading this correctly, we're supposed to take the river out of here."

"How are we supposed to do that, swim?" Garrett asked.

"Maybe he knows," Ryan suggested. He pointed to the last of the dwarves who was standing in front of a dock by the river. He was holding out his hand, palm upward.

"They still want something from us," Taylor Ann said.

"I totally forgot," Raegan said. She unzipped her backpack and took out the bag of treasure Garrett had placed inside. She hung the bag's drawstring on the dwarf's open hand and waited. Several seconds passed, but still nothing changed.

"A lot of good that did," Cade said.

How could it do anything? Raegan thought. *They freeze when we look at them.* "Everyone, turn around and close your eyes."

"Are we sure that's a good idea?" Garrett asked. "We did just give them a bunch of weapons."

Raegan looked the dwarf in his stone eyes. "I trust them," she said.

They all took several steps away and then turned around and closed their eyes. They heard someone rifling through Raegan's backpack, the sound of jingling coins, the tearing of a page, some scratching sounds, and other odd sounds they couldn't identify. It seemed to go on forever.

"What are they *doing*?" Ryan asked.

"Ryan, keep your eyes closed," Raegan replied.

"Ugh. 'Ryan look at the trees. Ryan *don't* look at the dwarves,'" he said mimicking his sister. "Why can't I just look where I *want* to look?"

They heard something that sounded like a pile of wood being dumped onto another pile of wood, then a loud plop and a splash, followed by several seconds of silence.

"It sounds like they're done," Taylor Ann said. "I think we can turn around now."

"Finally!" Ryan said.

When they opened their eyes, one dwarf had a snack pack and juice box in his hands. "I told you those snack packs were good!" Ryan said.

Garrett noticed one of the other dwarves was holding the plastic bag Raegan had filled with their trash. "They wanted our trash?" he said.

"Well, you know what they say," Taylor Ann answered, "one man's trash is another man's treasure."

"Who says that? Garbage men?"

"I'd rather have the treasure," Cade added.

Raegan noticed the head dwarf was holding a sheet of paper. She looked at it more closely and saw that he had drawn a portrait of her using her notebook. She took a pencil from her bag and wrote her name beneath the portrait. Then she put her hand on her chest as she looked up at the dwarf. "My name is Raegan," she said. "It's nice to meet you."

"Look!" Cade said. "A boat!" He pointed toward the end of the dock where a wooden boat was tied up.

"Where did that come from?" Taylor Ann wondered.

"Who cares?" Garrett said. "It's our way out of here."

Chapter 22: Down the River

As the kids loaded the boat, Raegan unzipped her gear bag and began putting on her wetsuit.

"What are you doing?" Garrett asked. "We have a boat."

"Boats sink and I want to be prepared. That's a river of wolf drool."

"The boat is not going to sink," Taylor Ann said, and not two seconds after she said it, the rest of the kids started putting on their wetsuits, too.

"Very funny, you guys."

"You have to admit, Sis, your track record is not all that great," Cade said.

Taylor Ann admitted it by sheepishly putting on her own wetsuit. Once dressed, they packed all their gear into the boat and hopped in. Everyone except Raegan who turned around to say goodbye to the dwarves. Only they were no longer there.

"Thank you again for helping us go home!" she shouted toward the darkness, hoping they could hear her. "Good bye!"

"Come on, Raegan, let's go."

They cast off the line and the boat slowly slipped away from the small dock. A few hundred feet down river, they entered a tunnel.

"What does the map say," Garrett asked. He and Cade were up in the bow, Garrett with a flashlight and Cade with an oar to keep the boat from ramming into the tunnel walls. Taylor Ann manned the helm—not that she was able to steer the boat anywhere. The river tunnel wasn't much wider than the boat itself.

Raegan studied the map before answering. "Up ahead, the river is supposed to split in two. We want to go to the right." She looked more closely. "We *definitely* want to go right!"

"Why do you say it like that?" Taylor Ann asked. Raegan handed her the map, and Taylor Ann looked it over. The path to the right was marked with the same O symbol they had seen in the tunnels. The path to the left had a picture of a sea serpent at the end of it. "Definitely to the right," she said.

Garrett noticed the tunnel walls were no longer rock. They looked like *ice*. He held out his hand to feel the wall and, sure enough, it was freezing cold. "Guys, I don't think we're inside the volcano anymore. I think we're in a glacier." They began going faster and faster until they were shooting down the river with furious speed. When they rounded the next turn, the boat rode up the side of the tunnel like they were in a bobsled race in the Olympics.

"Everyone, hold on," Cade shouted. He dropped the oar and grabbed the sides of the boat just as it took another turn. It went so high up the wall they almost flipped over. "We need to lean to keep from capsizing," he said after the boat recovered. "Get ready, another turn is coming. Lean right!" They all leaned to the right as the boat took the turn. "Left!" Cade shouted. "Right! Left!"

As they rounded the turn, Garrett realized the tunnel was about to split. "Go right!" he yelled to Taylor Ann, but it was no use. The force of the turn had swept the boat up the side of the tunnel and pinned them to the wall. There was nothing she could do to steer them to the right.

"No!" Raegan screamed as the river carried them into the left tunnel. The sea serpent tunnel!

Before they had any time to fear what would come next, the tunnel shot them out into a much wider river, and they heard a loud rumbling sound up ahead. Garrett aimed his flashlight to where the river seemed to just disappear.

"What is it?" Taylor Ann yelled.

Garrett turned around to face her. His eyes were so wide they looked like they might pop. "It's a waterfall!" he said.

Chapter 23: The Underground Lake

"Everyone, lean back and hold on!" Cade shouted. They leaned back so far they were practically lying down. "Get ready!" Cade said. "Here we go!"

The boat flew over the edge and hung in the air for just a moment before its nose tilted straight down and dove into the waters below. The boat hit the water with such force, Taylor Ann felt herself rise into the air before she smacked back down onto the boat's bottom.

"Is everyone okay?" Cade asked as the boat settled and began to drift.

"I am."

"Me too."

"Ryan?" Garrett asked. There was no answer. "Ryan?"

"Ryan!" Raegan yelled.

Taylor Ann searched the area around the boat until she spotted the faint green light of a glow stick sinking in the water. "There he is!" she shouted. Her Junior Lifeguard training took over, and without even thinking about it, she dove in after him. Garrett aimed his flashlight where he heard a splash and they all saw her swimming toward the green glow.

A few seconds later she broke the surface of the water with one arm around Ryan's chest and paddling back towards the boat with her other. When she reached the boat Cade and Garrett helped pull Ryan onboard.

"Ryan, are you okay?" Garrett asked. He gently smacked his face a couple of times. "Ryan!"

Finally, Ryan opened his eyes and coughed up water. "What a *day* I'm having," he said.

"Good job," Garrett said to Taylor Ann as she climbed into the boat.

"Thank you, Taylor Ann," Ryan added as he sat up.

"Are you okay?"

"Yeah. When I was older I did that all the time."

That made everyone laugh.

"Where are we?" Cade asked.

In response to his question, Garrett lit a flare and they saw they were floating on a gigantic lake inside a glacier.

"Not where we're supposed to be," Taylor Ann said.

"We missed the exit tunnel," Raegan said, looking at the map.

"What tunnel did we take?" Garrett asked. Raegan handed him the map. "Well that's not good," he said.

"Why? What tunnel did we take?" Cade asked.

"The sea serpent tunnel."

"What's a sea serpen?" Ryan asked.

"Like the Loch Ness Monster."

"Cool!"

"The dragon was small," Taylor Ann said. "Maybe the sea serpent is small, too."

"Or gigantic like the wolf," Cade said.

"Uh-oh," Raegan said. She pulled out her book on Norse mythology, flipped to the page about Jormungand, and handed it to Garrett.

"Oh, great," Garrett said.

"What?"

"Oh, nothing. Just a giant sea serpent that's so big, when he moves the whole Earth shakes."

"Well, that explains why the dwarves told us to go to the right."

Garrett scanned the lake. "There has to be a way out of here," he said. "Otherwise the water would rise to the top."

"Not necessarily," Taylor Ann said. "The glacier could be floating on the water."

"Is there any way we can climb up and go back?"

As the light from the flare started to die out, Cade noticed something was beneath the water. "Garrett, do we have any more of those glow sticks?"

"Yeah, a ton."

"Can you hand me a few?"

Garrett gave him a handful of glow sticks and Cade tossed one out into the water. He waited for it to sink to the bottom. "Do you see that? Something is down there."

"Yeah, a giant sea serpent."

"No, it looks like . . . " He tossed the other glow sticks in different directions and waited for them to sink. When they hit bottom, they created a faint ring of glowing green light. "It looks like there's a *city* down there." He turned back to Garrett. "The flashlights are waterproof, right?"

"Yeah, why?"

Cade just smiled and answered him by pulling his scuba gear out of its bag.

"Cade, you can't go scuba diving here," Taylor Ann said. "There might be something down there."

"Yeah," he answered. "And maybe *that's* why the dwarves wanted us to take the tunnel to the right. So we wouldn't find it."

"Find what?"

Cade's eyes lit up and he smiled wide. "Their treasure."

Chapter 24: The Treasure Below

Garrett and Taylor Ann began pulling their scuba gear out of their bags. "Wait," Taylor Ann said. "We can't *all* go." She nodded toward Ryan and Raegan.

"Okay," Garrett said. "You stay here, and Cade and I will go."

"Me? I'm the oldest."

"Exactly," Garrett said as he strapped on his diving vest. "You're the oldest."

"Mom and Dad don't ask *me* to babysit when they go out," Cade added.

"How are you even going to get the treasure up to the boat?"

"We'll take one of the gear bags."

"But it's going to be too heavy for you to swim it up."

She's right, Garrett thought. *I hate it when she's right.*

"I know," Cade said. "Give me your vest. And Garrett, hand me the rope and a glow stick." Once he had the rope, Cade tied it to the shoulder straps of Taylor Ann's vest. Then he tied the glow stick to the vest, too. He let all the air out of the vest, then dropped it overboard and fed the rope as it sank to the bottom. "We can tie the treasure to the vest and inflate the BCD to make it easier to lift. We'll pull it up once we're back in the boat. Plus, this will help us find the boat again."

"What's a BCD?" Ryan asked.

"It stands for Buoyancy Control Device," Taylor Ann explained. "It helps you sink or float when you're diving."

Raegan watched Cade tie the other end of the rope to the boat's cleat. "Are you sure this is a good idea? What if something happens down there and you need help?"

"The radios!" Garrett said. He searched his Uncle James's gear bag and pulled out the two diver communication units. He gave one to Cade, then he passed the hand-held radio to Taylor Ann. He attached his communication device to his mask and turned it on. "Testing, one, two, three, testing . . ."

"I hear you," Cade said. "Can you hear me?"

"*I* can hear you," Ryan said.

Garrett nodded. "I can hear you."

"So can I," Taylor Ann said.

"Wish us luck," Cade said as he sat down on the edge of the boat. He adjusted his mask and put the regulator in his mouth, then he grabbed the empty gear bag and held it to his chest before he leaned backwards and dropped over the side into the water.

"Don't stay down there too long," Raegan said to Garrett just before he dropped over the other side of the boat and into the water.

***

With the others gone, the lake was eerily quiet. Ryan leaned over the edge of the boat and watched the light from Cade's flashlight as he swam toward the bottom. "Do you think they'll find treasure?" he asked.

"Hopefully that's all they'll find," Taylor Ann said. It wasn't fair, she thought. She should be down there with them. Then she thought about her mother. Her mother was an experienced diver, too, but she didn't go out on the expeditions anymore. Instead she stayed home with her and Cade. Is that what being a parent means? Is that what being an adult means? Not always getting to do what you want, and having to make sacrifices for your family? She started wondering why she was in such a rush to grow up.

Ryan turned back and noticed Raegan was studying the wood engraving. He crawled over to have a look, and as he did, the boat began to sway.

"Please don't rock the boat," Taylor Ann said. "Nothing," she added into her radio. "I was talking to Ryan. Did you find anything yet?"

"Not yet," Cade answered over the radio. "We're about to reach the city."

*** *

As they swam through the water, Garrett felt like he was flying above the underwater city. It was much larger than the one from earlier—probably ten times its size. One half of the city was perfectly intact but sloped down at an odd angle. The other half was crumbling away into the water. It looked as if the city had fallen off a shelf and one half had smashed the other to pieces.

"There," Cade said, pointing to the largest building in the city. "That must be the great hall." He let the air out of his BCD so he would sink, and Garrett did the same. They landed in the middle of a large courtyard that fronted the great hall. Unlike the other city, this one looked old and decayed—all kinds of sea life were growing on the walls and, as a result, the buildings looked kind of hairy. The design of the buildings was different, too, as if they were from a more primitive time.

They swam up the steps of the great hall and approached the front door. The iron hinges were rusted and the door itself was warped and rotted. When Cade went to push it open, it simply floated away. He and Garrett entered and swam along the wall looking for an entryway into a treasure room. At the far end of the hall, they found a passageway with the symbol of a treasure on the wall next to it. Unlike the symbol in the other great hall, this one didn't show a maze around the treasure room.

Cade's smile appeared to fill his entire mask. "Ready?" he asked. Garrett gave him a thumbs-up and they entered.

***

"What are you looking at?" Ryan asked. He knew his sister was looking at the wooden slab the dwarves had given her, but she had been looking at it for so long, he had begun to wonder *what* exactly she was looking at for so long.

Raegan showed him. "There are more pictures on the side of the map, but I don't know what they're supposed to mean." One picture was of a boat, and another one looked like a small wooden box. There were words carved into the wood below each drawing.

"Can I see it?" Taylor Ann asked. Raegan handed her the slab. Taylor Ann looked at it for several seconds before she noticed the boat was starting to rock again. "Ryan, please don't rock the boat," she said, her eyes still on the wooden slab. "Just stay put."

"I'm not moving," he said.

The boat began rocking even more violently. Taylor Ann handed the engraving back to Raegan, and then aimed her flashlight at the waters around them. She saw small waves as if another boat had just passed by. They splashed against the boat. Just as the waves started to settle down, they came again, only this time from the other side. "Something is out there," she said. She flashed her light just in time to catch a huge, scaly-looking hump sink into the water.

Chapter 25: The Sea Serpent

"Guys," Taylor Ann said into the radio. Both her voice and her hand were trembling. "There is definitely something in this lake. And it is *not* small. "

"Is it the sea serpen?" Ryan asked. He could tell she looked worried. "Don't worry," he said. "I won't let it hurt us."

Taylor Ann nodded, but then caught herself. *Wait, was I just consoled by a five-year-old? What is going on here?!*

"Don't worry about us," Cade said over the radio. "We're inside the great hall."

The waves died down and the boat settled. "Is it gone?" Raegan asked.

"I don't know," Taylor Ann said. She got the creepy feeling someone—or something—was looking at them. She turned slowly toward the other side of the boat and aimed her flashlight at the water. There, sparkling in the beam, was a monstrous, scaly head with two gigantic, snake-like eyes resting just above the waterline. The eyes were watching them. Studying them.

Ryan crawled to the edge of the boat and jabbed his finger at the head. "You go away, Sea Serpen!" he shouted. But the eyes stayed right where they were. "Don't make me mad!"

The head sank slowly beneath the water. There was a long silence and they thought maybe the sea serpent had gone away, but then something smacked into the bottom of the boat and lifted it almost a foot in the air. They came crashing down on their bums.

"Where are you guys?" Taylor Ann asked over the radio.

***

"The treasure room," Cade said softly. It was hard for him to speak; the size of the room had taken his breath away. It was huge, as large as the great hall itself, and it was filled end-to-end with treasure. It would take his father's boat to haul it all away. Even the boat might not be big enough.

Garrett began filling the pockets of his scuba vest with jewels, and Cade did the same. When their vest pockets were full, they began stuffing handfuls of treasure into the gear bag. As he worked, Cade imagined his family sitting in the owner's box at Angels Stadium watching a baseball game. He couldn't stop smiling. They were both so overcome with excitement, they overfilled the bag and couldn't get it closed; they had to scoop out some of the treasure in order to zip it. It was too heavy to carry, so they dragged it to the door.

"How are we going to get it out of here?" Cade asked, looking up at the stairs.

"I know," Garrett said. He began inflating his BCD.

"Good thinking," Cade said as he did the same. With their vests fully inflated, the bag was much easier to lift.

"How much longer, you guys?" Taylor Ann said over the radio. They could hear the fear in her voice.

"We're on our way up."

***

The boat began rocking violently and Taylor Ann noticed the waves were coming from all directions. *He's circling us,* she thought. The waves died down, but that didn't bring her any comfort. The stillness was almost more unsettling than the waves. She scanned the surrounding waters with her flashlight, fearful of what she might find in the water. She heard it before she saw it. She turned and gasped at the sight of the sea serpent racing towards them at full speed. It lifted its head out of the water and opened its huge mouth like it was going to swallow them whole.

"I am *sick and tired* of this sea serpen!" she heard Ryan say. And then she heard a click and a swoosh and saw a spear shoot out and hit the sea serpent right in the nose. It let out a howl and writhed up into the air before crashing back down into the lake with a huge splash that sent water raining down on them.

Taylor Ann looked to the middle of the boat where Ryan stood holding the speargun. "In your *face*, Sea Serpen," he growled, unaware the shooting line was unspooling rapidly as the speared sea serpent swam further underwater.

"Ryan, let go!" Taylor Ann shouted.

The force on the line ripped the speargun right out of his hands, but not before pulling him smack into the side of the boat.

"Ryan! Are you okay?" Raegan asked.

Ryan rolled over. He had a huge bruise under his left eye. "What a *day* I'm having," he said.

"Good job, Ryan," Taylor Ann said and that made him smile. Just then, she noticed something pulling on the rope tied to the boat. "Cade, is that you?" she asked over the radio.

"We're tying up the bag," he said.

"Be careful. The sea serpent is out there." She looked over the side of the boat and could see his flashlight scanning the waters below.

"We don't see him," he said. "We're coming up."

***

After tying the bag of treasure to Taylor Ann's vest, Cade inflated the BCD to make the bag easier to lift. Then he and Garrett swam for the surface. With their vests fully inflated, they reached the boat in no time. They quickly climbed onboard.

"Did you see him?" Raegan asked. "He's *huge!*"

"I *speared* him," Ryan said.

Garrett chuckled at first, but when he saw Taylor Ann nodding, he asked, "Really?"

"Really," she answered.

"He saved us," Raegan added.

"Way to go, Ryan," Garrett said, messing up his hair.

"Come on," Cade said. "Help me pull up the treasure." He pulled on the rope, and as he earned slack he fed the rope back to Garrett and Taylor Ann so they could pull, too.

Raegan peered over the edge, her eyes on the glow stick tied to the bag, watching it slowly rise to the surface. It was taking forever. It was about halfway up when she saw a huge shadow approach the bag. "He's coming back!" she yelled. She watched as a giant mouth opened and swallowed it all— the glow stick, Taylor Ann's vest, and the bag of treasure.

"Ow!" Cade screamed. The rope slid out of his hands so quickly it caused rope burns.

Hearing his scream, Garrett and Taylor Ann instinctively let go of the rope. "What happened?" Garrett asked.

Raegan turned to face them. "The sea serpent ate the bag!"

The creature dove deeper into the water, dragging the boat down with it. Water began rushing over the bow as it submerged.

"Untied the rope!" Taylor Ann shouted.

"He's got our baseball team!" Cade shouted back. But since he hadn't mentioned his plan to buy the Angels to anyone, none of them knew what the heck he was talking about.

"He's going to pull us under!" Taylor Ann replied.

Garrett reached forward and tried to untie the rope, but the force on it was too strong to undo the knot. The boat began to creak loudly; it sounded like it was about to rip apart. With the bow submerged, the rear of the boat began rising into the air, causing Taylor Ann to slide forward. Just when they thought all was lost, the cleat the rope was tied to snapped off and went flying into the water. The boat settled, but it took a moment for the fear to leave them.

"Let's get out of here!" Garrett said finally. He handed Cade an oar and grabbed the other one for himself.

"Where?" Cade replied. "There's nowhere to go?!"

Chapter 26: The Way Out

Taylor Ann searched for a way out until she spotted what looked like a cave behind the waterfall. "Paddle for the waterfall," she said. Garrett and Cade paddled with all their might, but it was difficult because the current from the falls kept pushing them back. "Aim for the side," Taylor Ann said. They paddled for the side of the glacier where the current was not as strong, and then they made their way towards the waterfall. "See it?" she said. "There's a cave behind the falls."

The boat rose and dipped as the waves splashed off the glacier wall and churned underneath them. Finally, they overcame the current and slipped behind falls and into the cave. Once inside, the current pushed them back toward the far end of the cave.

Taylor Ann scanned the area with her flashlight and found a landing just as the boat smacked into it. "I want out of this boat," she said as she climbed onto the landing.

"Me too!" Raegan said.

Garrett climbed out after them. "Hand me the gear," he said to Cade who began handing him the bags one by one. Once everything was out of the boat, Cade picked up Ryan and handed him over as well.

"There's a tunnel," Taylor Ann said, shining her light on a small tunnel carved into the ice about three feet off the ground.

"What do we do with the boat?" Garrett asked.

"Leave it."

"But what if we need it later?"

"Pull it out of the water," Raegan said.

"We can't carry it with us, Raegan."

"Trust me," she said. She waited for the others to pull the boat onto the landing. It took all three of the older kids to lift it. Then she looked down at the wood engraving and tried to pronounce the words written beneath the picture of the boat. "Op . . . na . . . bá . . . tur," she said. Nothing happened. "Opna bátur," she tried again.

"What are you doing, Raegan?"

"Wait," she said. "I'm doing it wrong." She looked down at the words again. "Loka bátur," she said. At first, nothing happened and Raegan thought maybe she said it wrong again. But then the boat began folding in on itself, over and over again. It sounded like wooden planks falling on other wooden planks, and she recognized the sound from when they were with the dwarves by the river—after they had turned around and closed their eyes. When it was all done, the boat was the size of a small box, so small she could pick it up and put it in her backpack.

"How did you know it would do that?" Ryan asked, voicing the question they were all thinking.

"I didn't know it would do *that*," Raegan said. "But I knew it would do something. Otherwise, why would they give us the instructions?"

They felt a rumbling and then heard a loud splash come from the lake beyond the water fall. "Come on," Garrett said as he stuffed his gear into his bag. "Let's pack up and get out here."

Since he didn't have his gear bag anymore, Cade put his mask and fins into Taylor Ann's bag and his air tank into father's equipment bag. He left his vest on since there was nowhere else to put it.

Once they finished packing, Ryan pulled on his water gloves and clapped his hands together. "Let's do this!" he shouted, and then he turned and led the way up into the ice tunnel.

Chapter 27: The Ice Tunnel

The tunnel was too steep for them to walk up it. They had to dig their feet into the crevices and grab onto the knobs to climb up, which was difficult to do while also carrying their gear. It was a good thing they had their wetsuits on, otherwise it would have been freezing.

Not before long, their arms and legs began to burn and ache. Ryan was the first to say what they were all thinking: "Ugh. I am *sick and tired* of this ice tunnel!"

"Come on, buddy, we have to keep going," Garrett said.

"When you were older, you climbed this tunnel all the time," Raegan added in encouragement.

"That's true," Ryan said.

Just when they thought they couldn't go any further, they crawled out of the tunnel and onto a thin ledge overlooking a river.

"Do you think this is the river we were supposed to take before?" Cade asked.

They all crowded around Raegan who was looking at the map. "We went over the falls and into the lake here," Taylor Ann said. She pointed at the map as she spoke. "And then we climbed into the ice tunnel here." She moved her finger upward to where it connected to the other river tunnel, the one they were supposed to take. "I think this is it."

"It's not like we have any other options," Garrett said. "Okay, Raegan, it's up to you."

Raegan took the small box out of her backpack and put it on the ground in the center of the ledge. She took a few steps back, and then looked at the wooden slab. "Opna bátur," she said. The boat began unfolding.

Cade realized it was too big for the ledge and was about to fall into the water and be swept away. He rushed over and grabbed the boat's stern just in time. "Garrett, help me."

He was doing his best to hold onto the boat, but his feet were slipping on the ice.

"Ryan and Raegan, get in the boat," Taylor Ann said as she began loading their gear.

"Hurry!" Garrett said. "We can't hold it much longer." Taylor Ann loaded the last of the equipment and jumped into the boat.

"You go next," Cade said to Garrett. "I've got my vest on."

Garrett jumped over the stern into the boat, and the weight became too much for Cade to hold. The boat went rushing down the river, pulling him off the ledge and into the water. He held onto the boat for as long as he could, but eventually the force of the river ripped it right out of his hands.

"Cade!" Garrett shouted as the boat sped away, leaving Cade far behind them, floating in the water. Cade took a deep breath and began swimming for the boat, but it was going too fast for him to catch up.

"Use the oars to slow the boat down," Taylor Ann said. She and Garrett each grabbed an oar and began paddling backwards against the current.

"Swim faster, Cade," Raegan shouted.

Taylor Ann and Garrett were able to slow the boat just enough for Cade to catch up. He grabbed onto the stern and Garrett dropped his oar and reached over the edge to grab Cade by the vest. "I've got you," he said, as he helped pull Cade onboard.

"Well, that was fun," Cade said sarcastically.

"I want to go next!" Ryan shouted. He looked like he was about to jump overboard before Raegan grabbed him around the waist and pulled him back down. "Aw, c'mon! I can do it."

"I know you can, Ryan, but don't you think we've had enough adventure for one day."

"I guess."

"The exit!" Taylor Ann shouted. Up ahead, they saw sunlight streaming into the end of the tunnel. "We made it!"

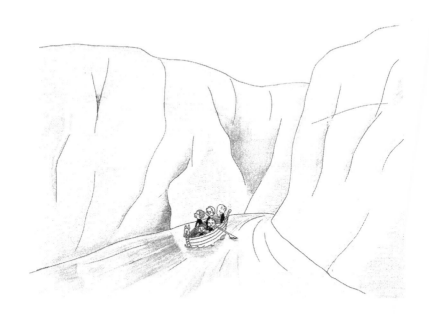

Chapter 28: The Glacier

After so much time in the dark, the sunlight was downright blinding and they had to shut their eyes against the glare. When they finally opened them, they found themselves on an enormous glacier. The river was flowing much more slowly now, giving them plenty of time to look around and take in the view. Huge walls of ice surrounded them on all sides. It reminded Taylor Ann of the Grand Canyon, only this was a canyon made of ice. Sunlight sparkled on the tops of the glacial cliffs, making them look like crystal. The river wasn't very deep and they could see the ice below it. The water itself was bright blue, like the water in a pool.

I should draw this, Raegan thought as she reached for her backpack.

As Cade took in the view, he became reflexive. "I can't believe we lost the treasure," he said. "Twice."

"Not all of it," Garrett reminded him. "We still have what we put in our vests."

"True," Cade said. He reached into his pockets to see how much loot was in there. *Not enough to buy the Angels,* he figured.

"What the—?!" Raegan said as she sifted through her bag. "Guys! We didn't lose *all* of the treasure." She pulled out the treasure sack she had given to the dwarf! "They gave this back to us!"

"Can I see that?" Cade asked. After he checked to make sure there was really treasure inside, he took the jewels out of his vest pockets and dumped them inside the sack with the rest of the booty. His smile was almost as bright as the crystalline ice. He handed the sack to Garrett who dumped his treasure in it as well.

"I have some," Ryan said, remembering the gold coins and jewels he had stuffed into his pockets. He crawled over to Garrett and dumped it all into the sack.

By the time they were done, there was so much treasure in the sack Garrett had a tough time tying it closed. He handed it back to Raegan. "Better put it back in your backpack just in case," he said. "Who knows what's going to happen next."

He no sooner said it when they felt a rumbling. "Oh, great," Taylor Ann said. "*Another* earthquake?!"

The river became choppy, tossing the boat from side to side, and the glacial cliffs began to make loud groaning sounds. Behind them they heard a thunderous crack and turned just in time to see a huge piece of ice break away and come crashing down into the river. The force of its splash caused a huge wave—a wave that was now rushing toward them. They heard more groaning and another piece of ice— this one right next to them—broke away.

"Paddle!" Garrett yelled.

Garrett and Taylor Ann each grabbed their oars and began paddling with all their might. The piece of ice crashed down into the river, right on top of the wave that was chasing them, and the impact created an even larger wave that towered at least ten feet into the air. All they could hear was the loud roar of the water rushing toward them. Garrett and Taylor Ann paddled furiously, but it was like paddling through river rapids. The boat kept rising and falling and a few times their oars struck nothing but air. The wave caught up to them and drove them forward with such force they all fell backwards. Far out in front of them, another large chunk of ice broke away and crashed into the river, causing another giant wave to form. It was headed right for them.

Chapter 29: The Final Escape

"Everyone, get down and hold on!" Garrett said. He waited for Ryan and Raegan to get down, and then he laid down on top of them.

"You're crushing me," Ryan said.

"Ryan! Don't argue."

"Here it comes," Taylor Ann said just before she ducked down herself. The two waves collided with such force the boat went flying up into the air. They hung in the air for so long they felt weightless, and Taylor Ann wondered what happened. She was about to look up when she felt the boat crash back into the river and water splashed over them from all sides.

Cade looked up to make sure everyone was okay. "Garrett," he said. "Hand me the oar."

Garrett passed the oar to Cade and then turned back to his brother and sister. "You guys, put your vests on just in case," he said. He pulled Ryan's vest out of his mesh bag and handed it to him, then grabbed Raegan's vest for her before pulling out his own vest and putting it on. "Taylor Ann, you want yours?" he asked without thinking.

"Yes. Unfortunately, a giant sea serpent ate it."

"Oh, right. Sorry."

There was a moment of silence before they heard more groaning. This time it was even louder. Whatever was going to happen next, the noise was telling them it was going to be something big! They heard another thunderous crack that echoed off the cliff walls. They looked around to see where the ice was breaking. Then the entire ice cliff on their right began sliding away from them.

"What's happening?" Ryan asked.

"Keep your head down."

As the ice cliff tore away, a huge gorge opened beneath them. The river itself stopped flowing forward and began to slide down the gorge, taking the boat with it sideways.

"Taylor Ann, we need to turn the boat," Cade said. Using their oars, they turned the boat to face forward just as it went sliding over the edge and crashed into the water below. "Is everyone okay?" Cade asked. No one answered, but he saw they were all still in the boat. The ice cliff was still in front of them, floating further and further away until they could see the outer edge of the glacier off to the side. "That way!" Cade shouted.

By the time they reached the end of the glacier and passed out into open water, Taylor Ann's arms were burning. They felt so heavy she could barely lift them.

Garrett could tell she was tiring. "You want to switch?" he asked.

As they switched places Cade took a moment to relax his arms and catch his breath. He looked back at the enormous glacier behind them. Chunks of ice were still breaking away and falling into the sea—too far away to hit them, but close enough to cause waves that rocked their boat.

After he settled in the bow with the oar, Garrett looked out toward the seemingly endless sea in front of them. "Now where?" He asked.

"I don't see land anywhere," Cade said.

Taylor Ann looked up to see where the sun was in the sky. "I think it's that way," she said, pointing to the distant horizon behind the glacier. "On the other side of the glacier."

Garrett and Cade turned the boat in that direction and began paddling. They did their best, but the sea was rough and the waves were tossing them around so much it was difficult to make any progress. They were starting to fear they might never make it around the glacier, much less make it all the way back to shore.

Ryan thought he heard a noise coming from his Uncle James's gear bag. He looked inside and pulled out one of the diving radios. He held it to his ear. "Hey, Uncle James. What's for dinner? I'm *starving*." The others all looked at him in confusion. "Don't get me started," he continued. "We just got off a glacier. It was totally falling apart. I dunno, how many glaciers are there? I only see one."

"Ryan, let me see that," Taylor Ann said. She took the radio from him and held it to her ear. "Dad?! Yeah, we're okay. We're in a boat out in the ocean. No, we didn't take a boat out, we—it's a long story."

"Where are they?" Garrett asked.

"They're in the boat looking for us."

"Tell him to look for the flare."

"Dad, we're going to fire a flare into the sky, okay?" She turned to Garrett and nodded, and Garrett shot the last of their flares into the air.

A long moment passed before Raegan saw something on the horizon. It was a boat headed their way.

Chapter 30: The Lost City

As her Uncle James's boat made its way toward them, Raegan kept her eyes on it the entire time, watching it slowly get bigger and bigger until finally it was close enough for them to tie their boat to its stern.

Ryan was the first to climb aboard. His mother was there to welcome him, and she noticed his swollen lip, black eye, and various scrapes and bruises. "Ryan, what happened to you?" she asked.

"You would not believe the day I had," he said, and without another word, he made his way toward food.

When they were all safe onboard, Raegan tugged on her Uncle James's shirt and asked in her soft voice, "Uncle James, can we take the boat with us?"

"I don't have any way to tow it," he said.

"That won't be a problem," Raegan answered. "It folds up into a box." She led him back to the stern, but when she peered over the edge, the boat was nowhere to be seen. "It's gone," she said.

"Where did it go?" Uncle James asked as he searched the sides of the boat.

"It must have gone back home."

"That doesn't make any sense."

"Trust me, Dad," Taylor Ann said. "There's no point in trying to make sense out of *anything* that happened today."

***

After the kids had filled their bellies with food, the adults decided it was time for some answers.

"Okay," James began as he sat down on the couch in the boat's cabin. "Why don't you kids tell me what happened."

The three older kids all shared a look that seemed to say, *How do we explain it?*

But before they could say anything, Raegan sat down next to her Uncle James and showed him the map she drew in her journal. "It started when we sank in quicksand and found ourselves in a cave with two tunnels."

"We took the dragon tunnel," Ryan added, sitting down on Uncle James's other side.

"But don't worry, the dragon turned out to be really small, like a dog."

"He likes snack packs," Ryan added.

"Not like the wolf. He was *enormous*. But I'll get to that." As she explained things, Raegan pointed to the relevant places on her map. "The dragon tunnel led us to a volcano where Ryan found another path that led to a diamond mine. And above the mine was their forge."

"Who's forge?"

"The dwarves. But I'll get to that."

"After the forge, we went into a huge stadium."

"Where gladiators fight," Ryan added.

"And next to the stadium was a castle. We had to climb up the castle wall to make it inside the city. And that's when the dragon chased us into a room with swords, and shields, and suits of armor."

"I fought one of them. That's how I got this bump."

"Then we went into the great hall. That's where we met the dwarves."

"We took their treasure," Ryan explained.

"But they made us give it back in exchange for showing us the way out. Then we went down this tunnel and across a bridge."

"That's where the dragon farted fire."

"And then through a forest of stone trees that kept trying to chase us until a glowing pig led us to the river. That's where we ran into the giant wolf."

"He almost ate Cade."

"But he was tied up with fishing line."

James looked to Cade who just shrugged.

"Then the dwarves gave us a boat, but we took the wrong turn and ended up in a giant lake with a sea serpent."

"I speared him."

"Beneath the lake was another city, and that's where Cade and Garrett found an even bigger treasure room. They put some of it in a bag, but the sea serpent ate it."

"He took your speargun, too."

"And then we climbed up an ice tunnel that led back to the river. And that river carried us out onto the glacier. But it started falling apart all around us."

"Worst. Glacier. Ever!"

"And then we made it out into the ocean, and that's where you found us."

Uncle James took a moment to consider everything she said. "Okay, very imaginative, you guys. Now why don't you tell me what *really* happened."

The kids all shared a look. Taylor Ann answered him by taking the treasure sack out of Raegan's backpack and plopping it onto his lap.

"What's this?"

"Take a look."

He opened the sack and pulled out a gold coin. He took several seconds to examine its strange markings. "Where did you get this?"

CHAPTER 30: THE LOST CITY

Raegan pulled out the wooden map the dwarves gave her and handed it to Uncle James. She pointed to the lake with the sea serpent. "Here," she said. "Beneath the lake."

He studied the engraving. "Where did you get *this*?"

"From the stone dwarves," Ryan said as if he was tired of having to explain it all.

"What stone dwarves?"

"The ones who live in the castle." Raegan flipped to the portraits she drew, and then handed her notebook to him. *It's a good thing I drew those pictures,* she thought as she watched her Uncle James flip through the pages, examining her drawings of the dwarves, the castle, and the great hall.

"I don't believe it," he said as he rose and crossed to a shelf. He pulled down a book, flipped through the pages, and then set it down on the table in the boat's eating area next to Raegan's picture of the great hall. They were almost identical. "It can't be," he said as he kept looking from one picture to the other.

"What is it?" Garrett asked.

"This picture Raegan drew looks like the great hall in the lost city of Sjór Borg."

"It's not lost," Ryan said. "The dwarves know exactly where it is. They live there."

James looked up at them, speechless. He turned to Taylor Ann for an explanation, but she didn't know how to make her father believe it. She could hardly believe it herself. So, she just smiled and shrugged.

"It can't be. People have been looking for Sjór Borg for centuries. The best explorers in the world have not been able to find it. And you just . . . *fell* into it?"

When he said it like that, it gave Taylor Ann chills. They did what the world's greatest explorers had failed to do for *centuries*. Okay, maybe they did discover it by accident, but they still discovered it. *And I'm only twelve,* she thought.

"I don't understand," he continued as he flipped through the pages of Raegan's journal. "If this is true, it means *all* the literature about Sjór Borg is wrong. How is that possible?"

"It's okay, Uncle James," Ryan said. "One day you'll be young enough to understand."

Made in the USA
Columbia, SC
28 June 2018